# Praise for
# Carlton Mellick III

"Easily the craziest, weirdest, strangest, funniest, most obscene writer in America."
—*GOTHIC MAGAZI*

"Carlton Mellick III h          titles... and the kinkiest fans!"
—CHRISTOPH          *The Stupidest Angel*

"If you haven't          enough
for the twenty first
—JACK KETCHUM, auu.

"Carlton Mellick III is one of biza.          , most talented practitioners, a virtuoso of the surreal, scie.. .ictional tale."
—CORY DOCTOROW, author of *Little Brother*

"Bizarre, twisted, and emotionally raw—Carlton Mellick's fiction is the literary equivalent of putting your brain in a blender."
—BRIAN KEENE, author of *The Rising*

"Carlton Mellick III exemplifies the intelligence and wit that lurks between its lurid covers. In a genre where crude titles are an art in themselves, Mellick is a true artist."
—*THE GUARDIAN*

"Just as Pop had Andy Warhol and Dada Tristan Tzara, the bizarro movement has its very own P. T. Barnum-type practitioner. He's the mutton-chopped author of such books as *Electric Jesus Corpse* and *The Menstruating Mall*, the illustrator, editor, and instructor of all things bizarro, and his name is Carlton Mellick III."
—*DETAILS MAGAZINE*

# Also by Carlton Mellick III

Satan Burger
Electric Jesus Corpse
Sunset With a Beard (stories)
Razor Wire Pubic Hair
Teeth and Tongue Landscape
The Steel Breakfast Era
The Baby Jesus Butt Plug
Fishy-fleshed
The Menstruating Mall
Ocean of Lard (with Kevin L. Donihe)
Punk Land
Sex and Death in Television Town
Sea of the Patchwork Cats
The Haunted Vagina
Cancer-cute (Avant Punk Army Exclusive)
War Slut
Sausagey Santa
Ugly Heaven
Adolf in Wonderland
Ultra Fuckers
Cybernetrix
The Egg Man
Apeshit
The Faggiest Vampire
The Cannibals of Candyland
Warrior Wolf Women of the Wasteland
The Kobold Wizard's Dildo of Enlightenment +2
Zombies and Shit
Crab Town
The Morbidly Obese Ninja
Barbarian Beast Bitches of the Badlands
Fantastic Orgy (stories)
I Knocked Up Satan's Daughter
Armadillo Fists
The Handsome Squirm

# TEETH AND TONGUE LANDSCAPE

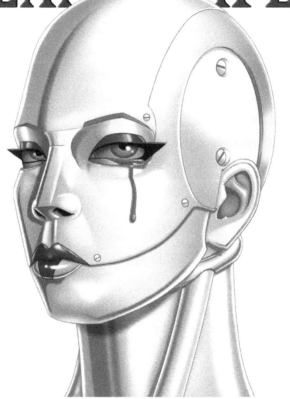

# CARLTON MELLICK III

ERASERHEAD PRESS
PORTLAND, OREGON

ERASERHEAD PRESS
205 NE BRYANT
PORTLAND, OR 97211

WWW.ERASERHEADPRESS.COM

ISBN: 1-62105-039-4

Copyright © 2003, 2006, 2012 by Carlton Mellick III

Cover art copyright © 2006, 2012 by  Ed Mironiuk
www.edmironiuk.com

All rights reserved. No part of this book may be reproduced or transmitted in any form or by any means, electronic or mechanical, including photocopying, recording, or by any information storage and retrieval system, without the written consent of the publisher, except where permitted by law.

Printed in the USA.

# AUTHOR'S NOTE

I don't remember writing this book at all. One day I found it on my computer buried in the dozens of unpublished novels I have molding there. I probably wrote it during a drinking/writing binge or perhaps my personality has split into two over the past few years and the other me is writing books behind my back. If I do have a second personality, his name is probably Laser Roboto. And I bet his favorite food is black licorice ice cream.

I guess I could use a second personality. One that knows how to drive a car and isn't afraid of grocery stores. My current personality utterly hates cars and grocery stores, which makes eating and getting places a bit difficult. I need to convince Laser Roboto to do those things for me. Did I mention he is from outer space?

Anyway, this story is set on a world made of meat. I mention this in the first line of the book, so don't think I just gave away the surprise ending or anything. I always wanted to read a book about a fleshy landscape but I haven't been able to find a single one ever in my life. So I guess that's why I wrote it. Perhaps it's just me, but I think all books should be set on worlds made out of meat. I have nothing against rocks and dirt, don't get me wrong, but flesh is just better. You can even make burritos out of it.

I'm eating a burrito right now. It's pretty good.

—Carlton Mellick III, 8/17/03 4:51 pm

# CHAPTER ONE

The world is made of meat.

It is not dirt/rocks/water anymore. It is flesh—warm, sweat-hairy flesh. A pop-twisting, pulsating, blubberball of a planet, mutating into slick deformities, leaking oil-tar acids and tangy metals. It grows claws of bone material like trees out of the ground, spider-reaching into the green cloud world to a cold/broken heaven.

I am lofty-running on the flesh dirt, pound-trampling bruises into its soft flab with my heels, no need for any shoes, rushing back from fishing at one of the wax-grease ponds behind Earth's mountainous left ear. I must get back there as soon as my legs can take me. No time to even examine the fish that I have just caught. I don't even know what species it is.

Well, maybe I can take a quick peek:

I have caught a plump mechanical fish, a cutter fish. It is both metal and meat. Edible, but very tricky to take apart. You need a screwdriver and wrench to disassemble the machine, to get to the food inside.

I need to get back to the city as soon as possible.

I have been all alone for over an hour and the lack of social interaction has turned me shaky.

I am nothing when I am alone.

I'm the only one in the city who eats the fish and animals living on the landscape. The others eat the meat of the Earth, plowing into it with rust-churning bulldozers, collecting flesh in the same manner they collected minerals from the sides of dirt mountains all those years ago. But I prefer to eat the cute wild animals, they are much more friendly to my tongue.

The city is just ahead:

A small cluster of sky-towers, five of them—cracks and black crab-vines creeping up and around their sides—five concrete demon fingers reaching out of the ground. And four letters are leaking out of the sides of my face:

H O M E

I can relax now. I am home.

I can even spell *home* backwards.

It is one of the words I have chosen to remember after books and writing left civilization. I feel very comfortable at home. It is where all the people in the world live. I write it in the sweaty meat ground when I bend over to catch my breath from running, cutting the skin with a hook and watching the words bleed. Of course, I keep the towers in the corner of my sight during the process of writing. I am so happy to be back. If it weren't for the friendly-tasting fish that live so far away, I would never leave my home at all.

I step into town, pass a well that centers the five towers, used for pumping blood and juices from the Earth, used for our drinking, cleaning, feeding the white toe-odorous fruits that grow from the Earth's hairs.

There is nobody outside. The wind hush-flows against the buildings and hair gardens and patchwork automobiles. People are always inside these days, hiding from the grotesque outdoors. I want to be inside with them.

The sky is going from green to red as I enter the only asphalt street on the landscape. The atmosphere has changed as well as the Earth. It no longer goes from day to night, white to black. There is no nightfall or daybreak. It goes from a world of green to a world of red.

Right now, redfall is upon us:

The deep bloody red swirls into the light lime green, making it swamp-like, eating its fluffy texture away. The red is heavy, sagging low to the flesh-surface, making crackles and squishy sounds as I enter my home tower.

Most people sleep during redtime. They are too intimidated to stay conscious. Its appearance is terribly distorted, rot-crazed. I can handle it some of the time, but I am definitely more comfortable indoors.

Within my home tower, I discover a dust-eerie silence. The silence slithering down from the stairs, curling around my ankles, slipping into my ears and mouth and nostrils.

The place is inert.

I tap the steps up to the second floor, wrinkle-watching for signs of life.

"Where is everyone?" I ask the sweaty walls, discarding my rod and cutter fish on a table-shaped tooth. The cutter fish squeak-flaps its metal fins.

I enter the first room I come across—all rooms look the same, with the same furniture inside, the same layout, the same familiar emotions—but the person is not here. Vanished. An old woman who is usually cleaning her clothes in Earthsweat at this time every day. Gone. I go to the other rooms, all of them empty. No sign of human life besides a strong aura of depression they left behind. And I have to hold myself up with a cane so that I don't become dizzy and fall down the stairs.

"What's going on?" I scream at the silence. "Where did you take them?"

I hammer-scurry down the stairs and into the street, glaring up at a demon cloud. It watches me like a bloodshot eye.

Charging through the quarter-mile of asphalt, I get to the city hall: a short and wide, curry-flavored structure made mostly of bone-bricks and metal wire-webs. The wire-webs stretch across the outside wall and are home to hundreds of mechanical spiders—shiny, metal creatures that are slightly larger than horse heads. Cautiously scratching my neck as I step through the threshold, knowing full well a bite from one could inflict paralysis lasting up to four days.

Inside the city hall, I discover a silence similar to the one in my home tower. But this silence is shrieking. It issues from a distant room. I follow the shrieking silence to the left wing of the building.

There are no people in sight, just shadows and a dull brown color-creeping. I need to find people. Quickly. I need to say hi to them and ask how things are going. It is making my eyes twitch like my eyelids have turned into sandpaper.

# CHAPTER TWO

I take a few more steps, slipping on all the grease that has been tracked in from outside, searching for some kind of life.

A flash of something passes between corridors.

It flashed by while my eyes were blinking, so I'm not sure if it is a real something or a fake something.

I call out, "Is anybody there?"

But the something does not show itself from the corridors.

I pray it is a child playing a game, or a councilman rushing busy through the halls.

My feet take me closer, the silence popping an eyeball in and out of my head, looking for something human.

Another spurt of movement scatters my vision, a shadow seeping from the hall out a window.

That one was real, I'm pretty sure.

"Please, somebody," I can hardly speak as I walk. My voice tight against my voice box like I am about to cry.

Rubbing my eyes of their burn.

There is something moving around in here, I can feel it, smell it. I don't think there is anything outside, not a thing, not anywhere in town. The towers radiate a flat and lifeless essence that I cannot describe, an anti-home feeling.

"I want the home feeling to come back," I say, ripping the greasy hair out of my skull.

A squeaky noise up ahead.

Yes, that was human-sounding. Someone *is* inside of here. The noise comes from the large conference room, the one where all the more-important people gather to speak about more-important things. But I do not hear speaking, only a squeaking sound like a mouse running up its exercise wheel.

"Hello?" I ask the squeaking, but it only responds with more squeaks. I can almost translate them into human words, trying to... imagining to, but it spins my head into hurting when I imagine too much so I cut that out quick and decide to take a look in the doorway.

There isn't anyone there. I haven't looked yet, but I already know. The squeaking is far too mechanical to be a human.

Stepping in the doorway, my eyes dizzy from imagining too much. There is nothing there. The squeaking is louder than ever, shriek-squeaks enveloping me.

"Hel—"

Wait a minute...

There is something in the room with me. That squeaking...

I focus my eyes a little clearer, into a corner by the window, my eyes cloudy from the outside red light piercing through the glass in my direction. But, wait... a brighter red is in the corner, two red dots...

Eyes.

Eyes, there are eyes looking at me, demon-like eyes. And they move toward me, closer to me and I see it clearly now.

A black creature. A black metal demon of a creature with glowing fire eyes and razor claws.

It pauses, examining me, making squeaky noises from its acid lips.

I wave at the creature, acting natural as if I knew it was going to be here the whole time. I can't show any fear.

"Hi," I say to it as friendly and anti-afraid as I possibly can.

And then I step out of the room and casual-hurry through the hall, speed-walking like I am late for a very important business meeting.

My mind is made up, I am fleeing from my home. I am not taking any belongings, none of the things that I will surely need. Not taking any chances with my life. Everyone else in town disappeared/died so easily, not putting up the slightest struggle. No, I will not be taking any chances with my life. It is all I have on me.

I am choking on something hard and prickly.

Running barefoot through the redtime fleshscape. The five fingers/towers growing smaller in the distance. Ahead of me there lies the sweaty plains, greasy mound-mountains in the distance, eye-digging loneliness in all of the directions forward.

Are there other communities still out here? During the past years, city after city would lose contact with us, with the towers, and we would just forget about them, let them drift to the backs of our minds so that we would have no worries. We have been all alone for the past year, no one for miles and miles to communicate with, alone with each other. Now I am alone with myself. And I know almost just as much about what happened to my friends and neighbors as I do about the other communities—they are all gone, just like that... as simple as drinking a glass of earthsweat, eating a bucket of earthmeat.

I am no longer running away. I am far enough from the evil black demon to catch a breath. The red sky crushing me into the ground with the palm of its hand, telling me to stop glaring at its bloody clouds or it will eat me alive.

I am in a scabby hole in the earth, a shelter, hard blood packed tight overhead. Throbbing warmth inside of here with me, fresh blood soaking my toes, but I cannot keep from shaking. I try to sleep but I am nervous. I feel like there are needles under my fingernails.

I do not understand the future.

Closing my eyes to avoid the red world and there is dark, soothing dark. I pretend the red does not exist. The red is dangerous. It makes me scared and I do not understand why I am scared. Fear is what is hard and prickly. I am utterly afraid right now.

My throat is choking on fear.

I am sick of being afraid.

# CHAPTER THREE

The bloody clouds begin to menstruate on me.

I am inside of my scab/shelter when the bloody rain comes down, flop-dribbling onto the fleshy ground that will soak it inside to replenish the veins. I catch a handful to drink, warm goo draining slowly down my throat. I cannot sleep and so I should eat. I need the energy. My face slimed over with sticky energy. My fingers adhering together. I am still choking. I am going blind because my eyes refuse to open.

The rain begins to pool outside the scab, streaming indoors and I find myself simmering inside of it, the wet-warmth possessing me, blanketing me in the physical and mental sense, forcing my twitchy body into rest. Smoothing out my nerves, my consciousness. I cannot keep myself from drowning into it.

The morning comes, a line of greentime light darting into my forehead, comforting enough to give me a smile. But the smile curls into panic as I notice that I am trapped inside of this scab shelter. It had scabbed over during my sleep and enclosed me within. Only a thin line of light enters through the crust.

I can move one arm and my head, the other pinned behind my back and both legs folded into the scab which had been fresh blood before I lost consciousness.

Try moving my legs... The flesh around them is stiff yet rubber-yielding, and so the scab shifts with my leg movements. But they do not let go.

I scream.

I don't know what else to do. There are no people around,

but I believe screaming is a good idea. It echoes in a lardy-strange way against the scab. Nobody outside at all. But I keep trying. Without help, I will surely die here. I am unable to help myself.

I scream. Pause. Scream again. I turn my throat into a sour mess. What if there are people out there but they can't hear me?

Can a scab be soundproof?

And as the question fingers its way through my dizzy-meated brain, I see a glowing red eye staring through the crack of the scab at me.

The eye disappears and I am alone again. I am not sure if I am relieved that the glowing red eye is gone or if I am worried. Either way, I am still trapped inside of this earth-scab and will need to begin screaming for help again.

But I do not scream. My throat is in too much pain. It burns, melting maybe, and my voice is gargling blood.

The eye reappears. It stares closer this time, to examine my soft flesh trapped within hard flesh.

And I begin to hear a hacking noise, the scab shakes around me. Staring through the crack and seeing only the greenness and a motion here and there, somebody trying to break through the cave to get to me. I am not sure what it wants to do with me. Save me? Kill me?

A metal hand-claw enters the small crack, made of wires and razorblades, digging a deep handful of scab and ripping it open, fresh earth-blood pooling all around me.

Crunchy-insect sounds outside as the something breaks through the scab, immersing me in a thick scent of hairy rotten beef, smashing apart into scab-dust showering the small space that I have and entering my mouth my eyes my lungs making it difficult to see/breathe.

The scab-dust continues its assault on my senses, even after

I have been freed from the scab. The razor hand seizing me by the arm and tearing me from that crusty place, cutting open the meat on my arm, human-blood mixing with earth-blood on the ground, and throws me to my knees before it.

Clearing my eyes of the scab-dust, looking up in the green-time light to see the metal-creature who is my killer or savior.

A woman.

She is made out of metal, mostly. In some joints there is flesh, or the illusion of flesh, but she is mostly made of wires and plates. Her eyes glowing red at me. Very human eyes, but are all bloody-red.

She doesn't say anything to me. Just standing there, wiry hair blowing in the green wind. The way her metal eyebrows curl upward and a fake smile of heart-shaped oily lips creating an expression that is salacious yet innocent, explaining to me that she is not at all dangerous in the way I originally imagined.

She still hasn't moved. Just staring down at me, blood dripping from her eyes like tears.

And I no longer feel alone.

# CHAPTER FOUR

"Who are you?" I ask the metal woman, but the metal woman doesn't seem to talk.

Her head cocks at me and twists around in a curious way.

"Where are you from?" I ask the metal woman.

She might not even understand me.

"You were the one in the towers, weren't you? You were the metal demon I saw, the one who scared me into the desert."

Her legs bending down twisty shoulders red eyeball curlings, to examine me closer.

Tiny teeth making a smile at me, confused over me but happy at me.

"Everyone at the towers disappeared and I thought it was your fault," I tell the metal woman. "I didn't know you were more a child than a monster."

She touches my shoulder, sizzling waves through my flesh, and she gasps in amazement, making clicking noises and eyeballing me up and down. She comes from a place of metal ones.

"Maybe you saw what happened to them," I tell her, asking the red part of her eyes. "I ran away too fast to investigate."

She touches the inside of my mouth, her metal both hot and cold, then clicky sounds.

"No, I don't want to go back there," I respond to the clicky sounds. "I don't want to disappear like the others."

Clicky sounds.

"Yes, let's go that way. I don't want to go back the way I came."

We walk for days and days, even through redtime, and my body becomes brittle-awkward from trying to trek on such fatty land.

The metal woman and I do not speak at all, but we relish each other's company. I can't handle the idea of being alone in the world. The metal woman has probably always been alone.

She smirk-glares at me with her demon eyes, walking with ease on the meat as I strain myself for just a few steps.

I stop.

"I can't go any further," I tell her.

Her head clink-twists.

And then, without warning, clouds storm in over our heads, barging right between us and then exploding with blood and guts rain.

A gooing, splatting storm. An intestine strikes like lightning.

We run to find shelter.

Over the next hill, the storm becomes unbalanced and drives the landscape insane. Veins popping out of the earth flesh, absorbing the blood and meat that falls from the sky, nerves squirming under our feet as if the planet wants to absorb us as well.

A giant beetle is up ahead, protected by the storm in its enormous shell. Its head is deep-digging inside of the earth, grinding into the underground arteries filled with the thickest and most flavorful helpings of earthblood, lightning/intestines striking its shell and falling limp on the ground.

I am exhaustion-falling over myself, legs collapsing me to the flesh. And the metal woman leaves my side.

She steps up to the large metal beetle and inserts herself into its big black rectum, cuts through him with her razor claws until her whole body disappears up inside of there.

I'm gagging on the blood that drains out of my jagged hair, my head folded onto my lap almost to sleep.

She has been gone for a long time. The beetle topples over, its head popping out of the earth to cause a geyser of black-purple blood, piles and piles of brown mush excreting out of the beetle's anus. The metal woman's body slowly creeping through the insect, fucking his guts out with her whole body, dumping them out.

She has been gone for so long, I am beginning to feel afraid and alone again, sitting in the soggy hairy patch of earth, bending a finger behind my ear.

When the last of the beetle meat has squirmed out of the man-sized anus hole, the metal woman comes sliming through like a fresh beetle birth, into the pile of guts. A click-clicky smile glows at me, won't stop glowing, and her hard-junk legs squatting into the mounds of beetle guts, scooping a clawful of that greasy muck and draining it through her shiny lips.

She click-clicks at me to come to her.

"I am not going to eat any," I tell the metal woman.

She clanky-runs to me and pulls me up by the hand, cutting my wrist a little. The smell of the beetle-fat on her makes my eyes water. And, clicking at me fiercely, she slides back inside the beetle's rectum, vanishing into the black. Her hand pokes outside, hard claw around my wrist.

And in one quick jerk, she pulls me in, sludgy shoulders, deep into the giant insect's corpse.

We have been here for weeks.

The hollowed out beetle shell becomes my new home and

the metal woman has become my wife.

She is still a stranger to me, this metal wife. She doesn't communicate like a human. She is close to a monster. Her attitude very child-like, but a monster still.

She has taught me hollowed-out beetles are comfortable little homes, twice as big as my old room in the towers. She has taught me to mold the fatty insect guts like clay to make furniture. I believe she was raised in a hollowed-out beetle as a little metal girl.

And the metal woman licks me with her gluey gray tongue.

She is like a cutter fish. I can unscrew the metal plate on her chest to get to the soft skin, pure white breasts with even whiter nipples. I smooth my hands over these delicate pieces of meat, tasting it with my sour tongue to make her go *click-click-click-click-click*.

And to make love, she opens a slot in her crotch for my penis to enter, hot oils dripping down my shaft, my thighs, sometimes my chin.

A few months pass and the beetle's body falls apart. While fucking today, her heavy body just crashes us both through the side of the beetle, loud smack against the blubber earth. The landscape ripples as we continue fucking on the ground, cumming against it.

It is early greentime, still a little red in the distance. It's been so long since we were out in the light, never knowing exactly whether it was green or red outside.

So cold. The green freezes all around me, wraps me up in needles, turns the warm sweat on me quickly to ice. And I spend many minutes warming myself up against the hot ground.

Clicky sounds.

"But where is there to go?" my voice muffled on the sweaty earth.

Clicky-clicky.

"I don't want to go that way.

*Clicky-clicky.*

"Fine, it doesn't matter anyway," I say to the metal woman, rising to get my clothes, to start another long journey.

# CHAPTER FIVE

The world has herpes here.

Pus-sticky grease between my toes, stepping carefully to avoid contracting herpes to my feet. I know how easy it is to catch diseases/infections from this planet. I know a woman who had them all up her leg, blisters like hair, gathering at her ass crack, swarming her vagina like frog legs.

"There is something over there," I tell the metal woman and she makes clicky sounds.

I take careful steps through the sexually transmitted disease field toward a something in the distance.

Look closer:

The something is a large steel windmill with sun-reflection blades, harvesting greentime light, singing to us in fairy hums.

The metal woman clicking at me, ripping into herpes, her toes without worries under plated armor. Glassy-whooshing as we up-up the hill. My metal wife is just too heavy to keep up with me on the slope, eyes steaming with frustration. Her arms reach out to me, calling me back to help her up, but I must see this windmill close up. I must see if there is a farm or perhaps a village nearby. A windmill is a sign of life.

Top of the hill:

Fields of genital warts stretch for miles past the windmill. I step carefully through the soupy meat, examining the terrain on the horizon. No sign of a farm, no sign of a village. Just a windmill.

"Do not drink the blood here," says a voice.

I turn to the voice, lips stretching a smile, there is life here!
... but I see no one.

Examining the windmill, it is a shiny metal structure reflecting its environment in such detail that there is not room left for detail of its own.

The metal woman reaches the top of the hill, click-crying for me to come back to her.

"Who is there?" I ask the shiny windmill.

There are shuffling sounds coming from within.

"Are you Themroc?" asks a voice.

"I am not Themroc," I tell a voice.

The windmill opens like a clam and a small person exits, paper skin and black tar eyes. I am not sure if it is a young boy or an old man. Perhaps it is both at the same time.

The child/oldman speaks, "I have not seen someone with a name other than Themroc in years," a curled chin as an attempt to smile.

"I am not Themroc," I tell him. I nod my head and the metal woman seizes control of my palm. "And this is my wife, a woman made of metal."

"It is good to see someone alive other than Themroc," says the child/oldman.

"Who is Themroc?" I ask him.

"I was once called Themroc," he says. "But I am no longer. I believed there was no one else alive in this world besides Themroc."

"My people were from the five towers that resemble fingers," I tell him. "Now they are all gone."

"Themroc must have taken them," says the oldman/child.

"I don't understand this," I say, smoothing my wife's shiny back.

"Come inside with me," he says. "You'll be my guest."

We spend long days with the oldman/child.

One night...

*Oldman/Child:* There are not things wrong with the planet Earth, there are only things wrong with Man.

*Me:* I don't know any things.

*Oldman/Child:* Where were you heading before you found my windmill?

*Me:* I was looking for the rest of the world.

*Oldman/Child:* There is nothing different in the rest of the world. Some of it is sweaty, some of it is hairy or has herpes and scabs. But it is generally all the same.

*Me:* I am looking for a civilization.

The metal woman grips my inner thigh with razor claws.

*Metal Woman:* Click-clicky.

*Oldman/Child:* Oh, more people... They are all gone, all of them. Only Themroc left in the world.

*Me:* You are not Themroc?

*Oldman/Child:* I was once Themroc. I am not anymore. I am still alive because I was/am Themroc.

*Me:* I do not understand Themroc.

*Oldman/Child:* There is a civilization called Themroc. Everyone in their community has the name Themroc. The Themrocs live in the valley between Earth's nose and mouth. They are the only civilization left in the world.

*Me:* What has happened to other civilizations?

*Oldman/Child:* The Earth wanted them all dead.

*Me:* What have we done?

*Oldman/Child:* You have become parasites.

It is our last evening we will spend at the windmill and the oldman/child is putting on a puppet show for our amusement, perhaps a persuasion to keep us from leaving him.

At first, I was thinking he would put on a childish act, a kid's tale of colorful characters and fun entertainment, something that would exhilarate his child-like features. But no, the puppet show is something that makes him more like a dirty old man.

We are cold faces watching the oldman/child as he crick-smiles at the two crude puppets made of meat and metal with enlarged genitalia forcing them to rape and mutilate each other. The oldman/child makes squishy noises for them, but there is no dialogue. No plot/story. Just a vulgar display of puppetry.

The metal woman makes clicky-clicky-clicky sounds like laughter, clapping metal hands and I try to keep myself from getting sick off the rotten meat smells which steam from the puppet stage.

I cannot eat the meal he has prepared for us. I am looking the other way and thinking about Themroc. Now I am plugging my nose and pushing the metal woman's fingers away from my crotch.

The red sky outside the window is crushing my face into the back of my skull and I can't think about anything anymore.

"Straight that way," says the oldman/child pointing into the valley to a dark city far-far into the reddish-green distance, prickly black structures along the horizon. The shadow from the earth's gargantuan nose blocks the color green for miles ahead of us, even though the closest nostril is at least a week's journey away.

"Straight that way," repeats the oldman/child.

I realize we have yet to begin moving, just staring off into the valley between Earth's nose and mouth. The oldman/child is not continuing with us past this point. He wants nothing to do with Themroc, or any other civilization. He wants nothing to do with himself.

The metal woman click-clicks in sadness as we walk away from him, grown used to his company, but the oldman/child is already going back home kicking flesh-dust into the air and sulking.

Into the valley of Themroc...

The metal woman's clawed toes are digging deep in the earth as we descend, clutching my body tight so that she doesn't slip and tumble down slope. At least the flesh is dry here, not sweaty/slippery.

*Me:* We'll find answers there.

*Metal Woman:* Click-clicky-clicky-click.

*Me:* No, we have to at least see what they are like. If they are the last civilization left on the world, we must try to become a part of them. Life is much more fulfilling if you are part of a community.

*Metal Woman:* Click-click.

*Me:* Don't be scared. Everything will be fine.

Her hand chokes at my neck, blood, metal eyelids flickering open and shut at the city in the distance.

The closer we get to the city of black pricky buildings, the more our hearts explode with mud-thick fluids. Screechy harp sounds emanate from the rubble and fences ahead. No signs of Themroc or moving things.

Something is wrong with my wife's sweat. It pools up inside her metal, collecting in vacant cavities, and once she is full of liquid tiny flaps open on her shoulders explode-spraying the sweat all over me. She just clicky-smiles at my soaked body, as if spraying sweat at someone is a way of flirting. The process continues every ten minutes.

Her kisses are hard against my face.

We enter the city cold and shivering, corpse-dragging ourselves through the dark blue ruins. Not a word from the city. Broken streets and buildings sinking into the earth-flesh. Mold and scabs grow up the dead structures. Everyone has disappeared from here, just like the ones from my old tower home, no movement/life. Thousands of people must have lived here before it was destroyed. So many high buildings that now shrivel-frown at the rubble below, rot-skeletons and meat vines, swarming stomach fruit.

"He lied," I tell the metal woman/wife. "Everyone is gone here too. Everyone in the world is gone. We are alone."

Clicky sounds and then she smiles at me, trying to pull me out of the city with her heavy fists.

"We need to keep looking," I tell her. "There is bound to be some answers hiding in this place."

Something to ease my mind.

# CHAPTER SIX

There is something moving inside of the city. I can hear noises in far off places. Trinkle sounds, humming metal sounds, and clanker sounds like animals digging through garbage cans.

"We are not alone," I tell the metal woman, smiling and scratching an eyebrow bloody.

The metal woman hears things I can't hear, but she doesn't tell me where the things are coming from. She cuts open the ground and rubs greasy blood all over her plates, struggles fingers through her joints and armpits to grease up the soft skin beneath the armor.

*Metal Woman:* Clicky-clicky-clicky-clicky.

*Me:* I can't understand you. The words are too fast.

*Metal Woman:* Clicky-clicky-clicky-clicky-clicky-clicky.

I am ignoring her, busy gathering flowers for the dead people in the city, bone-white flowers with meaty stems. It is socially correct to do this for people when you are the only one left alive. All of these people will be my friends once I die and meet them in Heaven. It is very social to believe in Heaven. Communities can be established just by believing in the same things. I believe in everything that everyone believes in. I make (made) more friends this way.

*Metal Woman:* Click-clicky-clicky-clicky-click.

*Me:* What is over there? I don't understand you.

I look over at her.

*Metal Woman:* Clicky-clicky-clicky-clicky...

But I don't need to hear anymore. I see it with my own

eyes: a metal jellyfish floats through the street to us, hanging from the sky by a long cord. Its tentacles are made of hooks and razor wire, its bell-body like a steel turtle shell with electric liquids bubbling out of it. The tentacles sparking as they rub against the asphalt.

*Me:* We need to go.

I charge away from the monstrous jellyfish. Just leave my wife in stares at the sparking street to save myself. It takes her a minute to realize I am gone. Her head tweaks and then she charges after me. Only she isn't fleeing from the creature, she believes I am trying to get away from her. She charges to capture me, crying and clicking, can't stand the thought of being without me.

There are more jellyfish lowering out of the sky, dripping out of the clouds umbrella-like, one large one just over my head. They were feeding on lightning up in the clouds, fully charged with electricity, crackling as they rub against one another, ripping through the green air to us.

They want to cause us pain. They want to eat us, or kill us and chop us up for their babies to eat.

They want to touch the metal woman and electrocute her, make her pop open like crab meat. They want to hook our mouths with long electric pubic strands, hair/arms. They want to pull us up into their metal wombs.

The large one descending on me:

I look up into it...

There are people up there, inside of its bell. People trapped, paralyzed, still alive but unable to free themselves.

Cutting my arms and legs, tentacles are wrapped around me. Lifting me off the ground. I try to resist, twisting a tentacle backwards. It refuses to let me go.

The people inside of it look lonely. They are crammed in so close to each other, like a loving family by the fire, but they look like strangers to each other. Alone together. They have nobody but the cold metal fish, enslaved by its stomach. They look like they've been digesting inside of it for a thousand years.

The jellyfish tentacles begin breaking apart, freeing me.

I come out of a long daze.

The metal woman is attacking the creature, leaping from the ground and clawing its tentacles to shreds. Sparks are flying and the people inside of the jellyfish's bell scream at me, drill-crying in agony as if their nerves are connected to the creature's.

The metal woman springs dozens of feet in the air, cutting open the body of the creature, electric explosions, raining bits of fire. But the jellyfish will not let me go. It falls from the sky, collapsing to the rubble streets, but I am still entangled in one strong tentacle.

It dies slowly. I close my eyes and try to sleep. My head is dizzy. I open my eyes again to see all of the faces inside the jellyfish staring back at me, blank expressions.

"I can't take you with me," I tell them. "You are no longer human."

I want to cry for them. I force myself to. I bite my lip until tears fall from my eyes and then pretend to be sad for them. They probably like me better now that I'm sad for them.

# CHAPTER SEVEN

The jellyfish do not follow us beyond the city. We continue on our path toward the Earth's mouth, searching for signs of life. The metal woman exhausted from saving my life. She can hardly walk straight anymore.

After an hour of travel, we discover human life. But instead of feeling joy I feel disgust and pain:

Over the hill, we see a woman being murdered by two men.

We move in closer.

She is being cut apart with sharp rocks by the two men who seem to be identical twins.

We move in closer.

The twins are identical in every way. They attack her in unison, stabbing her to a sort of rhythm.

Closer.

The identical twins are both oldmen/children. Like the man who runs the windmill. Except these two have togetherness and the windmill man was alone.

They must be Themrocs.

"And who might you be?" the identical oldmen/children ask me. All I do is point to the name tag the windmill man gave me.

Written on the tag are the letters:

T, H, E, M, R, O, and C.

"Hello, Themroc," says the left identical twin.

"You have been gone for so long," says the right twin.

The Themrocs are at once my friends and we smile and shake

each others' hands over and over for a good ten minutes. Neither Themroc, left or right, seems to notice the metal woman beside me.

They just clap their hands in a criss-crossy pattern and take me, along with the lady's corpse, back home with them.

And the metal woman drips oily tears at me for not paying very close attention to her at all times.

The Earth is very shifty here. It seems to vibrate and roll around whenever it wants to. Lots of spine-bushes and slime gatherings are here.

*Themroc:* The sky is a nice shade of forest.

*Themroc:* Yes, God must be in a decent mood today.

*Me:* It is a much better color than red.

And both Themrocs glare at me with crooked faces.

We arrive into a gathering of maybe twenty or thirty Themrocs, all of them identical in every way, near a giant mouth on the ground, Earth's mouth. They are feeding non-Themrocs to the Earth.

*Metal Woman:* Clicky-clicky-clicky.

The ground opens up, giant gooey lips spreading and Earth's ocean-sized tongue slips out of the ground at us. The Themrocs I arrived with ask me to assist them in placing the dead woman on the tip of Earth's squishy tongue.

*Themroc:* Mother Earth prefers her food alive.

*Themroc:* Food is much better that way.

All of them nod.

"It's been a while, Themroc," say many of the Themrocs to me when I pass them, always looking at my name tag and never my face. One glance and they'd realize I look nothing like them. They'd discover I am human. Are Themrocs human?

The metal woman click-clicks at them and makes twisty sounds around me. They ignore her. She is invisible to them.

Themrocs load the Earth's tongue with living humans, families of people with facial expressions like blank pieces of paper, perhaps hypnotized as the ocean of tongue slides back into the Earth. The people sinking into the wet darkness, fat hill-lips squeezing around them, swallowing them deep under the ground to nourish its flesh.

All of the human prisoners of the Themrocs have faces like blank pieces of paper, all in cages and waiting to board the tongue to feed the planet.

The metal woman clicks to herself, mad at me for not acknowledging her.

*Themroc:* They are so delicious to Mother Earth. She just loves human food so much!

The metal woman cannot stand for me ignoring her any longer and grabs me, holds me, nuzzles her hard steel chin into my shoulder. I try to push her away, scared a Themroc will see, but she is too strong.

The Themrocs look in my direction, but see nothing out of the ordinary. They just smile at my name tag and wave.

By redfall, all the humans in the world are gone, eaten up by the Earth, dissolving in the stomach bag which is also called Hell. I secretly denounce my humanity and accept that I am a Themroc. So the human race is truly dead now. Only Themrocs and metal people remain.

Taking us indoors:

A home that is a giant box, a building/treasure chest, miles high. It has only one entrance and the walkway to this entrance is a velvet red carpet.

*Themroc:* Today we are going to have a feast, celebrating the death of all humans. We have finally saved our loving planet from evil human ways.

I smile at Themroc, nodding my head excitedly. A celebration sounds fabulous! I can't wait for my first Themroc social event!

... though, as a human, I am in mourning for my people and do not find their ultimate demise a happy occasion to celebrate. But I do feel like celebrating my new found community. I am no longer alone.

... well, perhaps I *am* happy that all of the humans are dead. I am a Themroc now and Themrocs are happy that the humans are dead. So, yes, I should be in a very cheerful mood and not in mourning. I am much more happy when I am happy than when I am sad.

# CHAPTER EIGHT

Before the festivities, I wander the fantasy rooms of Themroc Manor with my metal wife going clicky-clicky-clicky all the time. She holds my hand so tight that it bleeds.

The walls in here are gigantic, bigger than my whole life. There are twenty floors, each one with a ceiling miles high.

*Themroc:* We have an entire world inside our home.

And Themroc wasn't exaggerating. One section of the house is Brazil. Another section is Mexico. Antarctica is in a ballroom. Africa is hanging from the fourth floor ceiling. It is as if all the colorful parts of what used to be the world were taken off the Earth's surface and stored inside of here, just before the planet changed from soil to flesh.

*Metal Woman:* Clicky-clicky.

She is pointing at tiny metal people crawling inside of a tiny model of New York City in one chamber. She pokes me, clicking, looky-looky at me. They are not metal-plated people like her. They are mechanical toys. They were created by Themrocs to make their model more fun. My metal wife doesn't realize this. She points and pokes me. Clicking, clicking, clicking.

*Themroc:* The world's beauty is all here, intact. But there are no humans here. There are signs of human life, products of humans, such as the pyramids and bridges and monuments, but there are no longer any humans. They were ruining nature and so nature changed itself. It turned into flesh. The world was once beautiful, but now it is ugly. Flesh is ugly. The Earth went from being selfless/providing to ugly/murderous. Thousands of people have to die every day to feed one belly. That is pure ugliness. It is murderous gluttony.

*Me:* What will the Earth eat now that the humans are gone?

*Themroc:* The Earth must become vegetarian.

I cannot stop smiling.

My new home is amazing. It is full of life and social activity. My smile gets bigger and bigger.

I enter my bedroom. It is dirty and very small. The metal woman bounces on the bed rising dust into my lungs, blinds me. It might be a sad room compared to the rest of the mansion, but it is enough for me. I'm just happy to be a part of the Themrocs.

Well, maybe I am a little unhappy with the room. It is too anti-social. Guests would never visit my bedroom. It is hidden in the dark sections of the manor, where black tarantulas play.

I sprawl out on the gritty bed. The metal woman curling around me with her cold hard skin. I slide a finger from her shoulder down to the smooth plates on her back, kiss her neck.

She click-click-clicks, placing a screw driver and plyers on the bed between her legs, waiting for me to open her up and get inside her shell.

Time drifts and we have yet to eat a thing. The metal woman cuts a hole in the carpet, but cannot find any blood. She doesn't understand why the floor is not made of meat, cries with frustration.

We wander into the hall and I sing a nursery rhyme to her. Nursery rhymes always cheer her up.

Click-click-clicky.

37

*Me:* Is it time to eat yet?

*Themroc:* I should be asking you this question.

*Me:* I have just arrived here from far away.

*Themroc:* Yes, we know you have been away, but we were all under the impression that you would be providing us with dinner.

*Me:* I do not understand you.

*Themroc:* You bring your turkey around with you. We figured you were planning on giving us a feast.

*Me:* I don't have any turkey.

*Themroc:* But it is behind you.

I turn and see only the metal woman standing behind me.

*Me:* You can't possibly mean my wife?

*Themroc:* Wife? This is food.

*Me:* This is not even similar to food.

*Themroc:* If you don't feel like cooking, just hand it over to me. I am the Themroc who cooks.

The Themroc who cooks reaches for my metal woman, but I push him away.

*Me:* Don't touch my food!

My fists raise at him.

Themroc laughs at me, as if I'm a joker, and he takes the metal woman away from me. She click-click-clicks as she is pulled into the distance, but I do not stop the Themroc.

I love her so much, but I can't save her. Themrocs will probably think ill of me if they discover I am in love with food. It would definitely be death to my social life. And life is worthless without a social life.

I can hear her clicking across the mansion, until she is taken to the kitchen.

Then there is no more clicking.

# CHAPTER NINE

The metal woman's shell is in pieces across the dining room table. Themrocs lick her meat out of her metal on their plates, dipping loaves of cracker-stale bread into her greasy sauces.

It disgusts me to eat her, my wife who loved me more than the whole world. But I need to fit in with the Themrocs. It is very important that I fit in. I try to eat more than anyone else. To make them proud. Also, I want to eat more than the others because I know she would prefer to digest in my stomach than any of the other Themrocs.

*The Themroc who cooks:* She does not have a soul. Animals like her were made for meat.

Her meat stares at me from my plate, her vagina meat and some breast meat, a nipple like an eyeball. My finger caresses the flesh with a knife, cutting tender pieces and sucking it into my mouth. A stringy flavor.

I wonder if she was pregnant with my child. Perhaps she was. Perhaps there was a little fetus growing inside of her, and one of the Themrocs is gnawing on it right now. I look around at everyone's plates, but there are no signs of a fetus...

There is very little dinner conversation. The silence makes my eyes twitch.

The seat at the end of the table is empty. The metal woman's head rests on the plate in front of it, eyes closed like she is only napping, like she would do against my thigh. I can picture those eyes opening up at any moment, heavy-cold arms wrapping around me, click-click sounds vibrating through me like purrs.

It would have been a mistake to turn down the Themroc who cooks. I would have had to flee from their home with the metal woman, to a dark and lonely side of the world. She is horrible company. She can't even speak right. Two people do not make a community. You need at least a dozen.

After dinner, the Themrocs who clean must do their duties. I soon discover that I am one of the Themrocs who clean.

We collect the greasy plates and silverware, the empty shells of my metal woman, and I am sent to a small gray section of the kitchen to wash the dishes with another Themroc who dries the dishes.

The sink is a bubbled black metal bowl, filled with a green liquid and fishy smells.

"What Themroc did not show up for dinner?" I ask the Themroc who dries dishes.

*Themroc:* All Themrocs were at dinner. We usually are short one, but now you have returned.

I hand him a dish to dry.

*Me:* But the chair at the head of the table was empty. There was food set there for someone. Who was it for?

*Themroc:* That food is for God.

I hand him a dish to dry.

*Me:* Oh, it is a religious thing. You leave some food to your god like a sacrifice, right?

*Themroc:* No.

His face is confuse-wrinkled.

*Themroc:* God needs to eat, just like Themrocs.

*Me:* But you never see your god, do you? He is just a belief.

*Themroc:* Of course we see Him. He lives upstairs.

I hand him a dish to dry, but won't let go once he grabs it.

*Me:* What do you mean?

*Themroc:* He lives in the uppermost floor.

*Me:* Oh, you mean in Heaven.

*Themroc:* Yes, we are in Heaven.

I let go of the plate. Themroc dries it and places it onto a wire cart next to him.

*Themroc:* God hasn't come down to dinner in quite a long time. We are all worried about Him. Something must be troubling Him greatly.

*Me:* ... Did you say we are in Heaven?

*Themroc:* Yes, we are in Heaven. This is God's home.

*Me:* Heaven is supposed to be in the sky.

*Themroc:* Heaven is wherever God wants it to be.

*Me:* So where are the angels?

*Themroc:* We were created by Him to be His servants. You certainly have been away for a long time, Themroc.

After I am excused of my duties, I saunter out of the kitchen to the dining hall. The room is very dim, lit by a single candle at the end of the dining table in the seat where God was supposed to sit. The cleaners did not take His food away. His plate is still in place. My metal woman's head is still lying peacefully on her cheek.

I stare at it for several minutes and then step forward, lying my head on the table to gaze into her eyelids.

"We are together in Heaven," I tell her.

I smooth my palm over her cold metal forehead.

"It won't be the same as before, but we must try to make it work. You belong with me. And I belong with Themrocs."

I take her head from the plate and hide it under my shirt, creeping quietly up the cloud-world stairs to my bedroom.

Halfway up the stairs I am greeted by two Themrocs who will not let me pass. They introduce themselves as the Themroc who sews and the Themroc who paints. They ignore the bulge in my shirt, as if it is normal for a Themroc to be pregnant with a metal woman's head.

*Themroc:* The morning dog requires all of your attention this evening. He will be coming around to your bedroom at 9:00 for petting and to be scratched behind the left ear. Do not feed him greasy foods for this makes him fat and lazy. The morning dog must visit twenty-four bedrooms every day, so do not slow him down.

*Themroc:* If the morning dog does not arrive, you will understand that the world has ended and you have only the rest of the evening to take care of small personal obligations before your expire.

*Me:* I don't want the company of a dog.

*Themroc:* It is your most important duty as a Themroc to pet the morning dog. You have gone without petting him for many years. The morning dog has been lonely for you.

*Themroc:* You will not be welcome here if you refuse.

# CHAPTER TEN

The morning dog visits my bedroom while I am painting a picture of all my fellow Themrocs on the wall above my bathtub. I was given permission to do this from the Themroc who paints.

*Themroc:* It is permitted, but no one understands why this interests you.

There is a knocking at the door and enters the dog. The dog is low to the ground and made out of leftover body parts, human flesh sewed together into a patchwork dog. A baby's arm is wagging as its tail.

"You can sit over there," I tell the morning dog. "I'll be just a moment."

But the morning dog just stands there, panting, wagging its baby arm/tail, excited for me to pet him and scratch his ear.

It is quite a grotesque species of dog. Just the thought of caressing its furless skin is offensive. Pets are supposed to be cute and fuzzy, but this creature is crawling with ugliness. There would be no satisfaction in feeding it any of my affection.

How can the Themrocs pet this monster every night? Do they enjoy it or do they just do this out of necessity?

It is still staring at me, wagging its tail and panting. It whines, shifting side to side on its flabby legs.

I put my paints down and approach the morning dog. It is now excite-hopping side to side at me, awkward movement as if it is ready to fall apart in front of me.

Eyes closed:

I reach my hand for it and squish into sweaty skin. My fingers fiddle against it, petting in quick and clumsy strokes.

Open my eyes: the morning dog is happy-huffing at me. It licks my hand and then forces his left ear against my fingernails to scratch. A rotten-melon flavor wells from its wet parts.

Escorting the morning dog out of my bedroom, I tremble-mutter some words that are supposed to be "goodbye, see you tomorrow," shaking the baby-arm/tail on its way out.

I can't sleep very well tonight. It is my first day in my new community, which happens to be Heaven, and I am nervous of what the Themrocs think of me. They are so much different than me. I don't fit in at all. Perhaps I am too curious. Perhaps I am being too human. They are a very private people.

The metal woman's head is on the pillow next to me. It doesn't make any clicking sounds like when we'd sleep before. The clicking used to put me to sleep like a cat's purr.

I fall asleep and I wake up. I can't sleep again. Stepping down from the bed, I wander the extravagant halls of Heaven, examining the glorious landscapes that decorate our home.

*Themroc:* What are you doing out of your bedroom?

I turn around to find a Themroc raking leaves in a forest nearby.

*Me:* I want to see God.

*Themroc:* Yes, He is usually about at this time.

God is creeping naked through the museums inside of Heaven, investigating His memories to keep His mind off of work. He is a very pale/flimsy old man. His flesh appears glued to his bones.

I follow through the halls to enter conversation with Him, to find out what's wrong.

"It is no use, Themroc," God says from the distance.

I pause, staring at the crumple-skinned man.

"Excuse me?" I ask Him.

"I cannot be cheered up by you. I have damned myself to this prison and you do not have the wisdom to help me." Staggering through His memories, drunk and senseless.

Even God thinks I'm really a Themroc...

"I am not here to cheer you up," I tell God. "I just want to ask you some things."

But the old man is weeping and lost inside himself...

# CHAPTER ELEVEN

Weeks go by, maybe months. I am no longer happy with my life.

Satisfaction in my present situation has faded and I cannot understand why. Perhaps because I still do not fit in? That would explain everything. I must fit in. I spend all of my time now trying to fit in, be more like Themroc, live up to my name tag.

The daily schedule of Themroc consists of polishing small translucent blue marbles and looking through them at each other. Then they will eat a meal and discuss what is inside the marbles. And then they go back to staring at the marbles.

I cannot see anything when I look into the marbles. I try to be a Themroc, shining up the marbles I was given and staring at them for hours, but there is nothing. I just see blurry glass. This confuses me and I don't understand why they are so important to Themroc. This is the only entertainment Themroc has to offer.

When Themroc asks what I've seen in the marbles, I shrug and say "mine are all boring ones" and Themroc says "yes, there are a lot of those in the bunch."

And I try to change the subject as quickly as possible.

I figured that God would make much better company than Themroc, but I was very wrong. He is usually very hard to find, and once you find Him you'll feel a deep wave of depression pushing very hard at you. So hard that you just want to leave Him as quickly as possible. Run away from Him.

I sometimes go to His room to be friendly. I bring Him some warm beetle mush in its shell-bowl.

But He says, "No, I'm too tired to eat."

And so I make a bed of feathers and pillows shaped like cozy-hugging arms and chests.

But He tells me, "No, I am too hungry to sleep."

And so I re-offer the bowl of beetle food.

"I'm too tired to eat," He tells me.

So I re-offer Him the bed with the addition of a tree-skin blanket.

"I'm too hungry to sleep!" He screams at me, tossing His Big Book at me.

Then He crumples the papers on his writing desk and throws them at me one by one.

*"You should not go outside alone. The world is a harsh place of wild mechanical animals and demons,"*—a sign on the road outside of the treasure chest.

Stepping the velvet walkway through the wasteland outside of Heaven:

I'm holding the metal woman's head at my waist, rubbing fingertips into the soft eyes. Still moist and drippy. I can hear the screeching jellyfish in the city in the distance. They are crying out for me to come live with them, inside of them. But I do not dare approach.

A week or so ago I had a conversation with one of the Themrocs who clean...

*Me:* What city is that just outside of Heaven?

*Themroc:* There are no more cities.

*Me:* It was once a city. What was it called?

*Themroc:* It was never a human city. It is where all the Demons live.

*Me:* I think I was attacked by a Demon.

*Themroc:* The Demons are brothers of Themroc, but we do not keep company. Both of us are collectors of human souls, only Themrocs keep their human souls in tiny marbles and Demons keep them partially alive inside of their bodies, like food in their stomachs that will never fully digest.

*Me:* Do Demons prefer the souls of evil humans and do Themrocs prefer souls that are good?

*Themroc:* Of course not. There is no way to separate good from evil.

Stepping off of the velvet path and onto the flesh ground. I wander through prickle bushes and gluey meat rocks, gathering flowers from the bone trees. Hopefully the Themrocs will appreciate these flowers and gaze or smell them for hours at a time. They will love me for my gesture. They might make me honorary Themroc.

Wet-warmth rises through my flesh as I enter the land near the world's mouth. Its deep sleepy breath churshes through the atmosphere, giant lips like crusty mountains that begin to chip, irritating the Earth into sticking out its enormous black tongue and licking up the scabs around it. And I have to be careful not to get swept up into the deep hole.

Its massiveness begins to creep up on me. I hear the ground shaking and I see its huge taste-mounds bearing down, itching to taste me...

But it stops. It turns and licks in the other direction. Then falls back inside its lips.

"You see that," I tell the metal woman's head. "Themrocs are respected by the whole world."

Her response is a black silence.

# CHAPTER TWELVE

The biggest flowers I can find come from bushes larger than Earth teeth. There are mountains of these bushes in the distance, spread across the landscape like an army.

"These will make the Themrocs kiss me all over," I tell the metal woman's head. "I will be the honorary Themroc!"

Arriving to the flowers:

They are open to the world as if awaiting to be embraced. Trudging through sweat to pluck them into a collection. But inside of a flower, curled inside of the petals, I see a hard black ball.

"These aren't very pretty," I tell the metal woman's head.

I can tell she is as disgusted with the flower's insides as I am. The black lump looks like a tumor inside of the beautiful blue-pink-purple flower.

"Let's see if we can't remove the tumor without ruining it," I tell her.

I grab hold of the ball and tug. It is as hard as steel and won't let go. The tumor unravels in my hands, stretches out and pushes me away. The tumor is something alive. I immediately think it is a large insect until the thing begins to cry.

Its squealing and scared-clicking sounds are very familiar to me. The black ball is a baby metal woman and it is seizuring the beautiful petals, thrashing its little arms and legs. Then all of the other flowers begin thrashing with metal babies. An army of squealing cries shudders the fleshscape.

I back away from them. The pitch of their screams makes me unsteady. Then the metal people appear.

They step out of the flower bushes to me, angry clickings at me. And they focus all their eyes at the metal woman's head in my arms.

So I run. I turn, dash away. Pounding bruises into the blubbery ground.

The metal ones chase close behind me. They are too heavy to keep up, but very determined to catch me. I can feel them swinging their claws, cutting plants out of their way to get me.

The ground is sweaty and slippery. My sense of hearing has cracked, the angry clicking sounds have become white noise.

Once I reach the velvet walkway to Heaven, I feel I am safe. But the metal people are still behind me.

They won't dare approach Heaven. Themrocs are masters over the barbaric metal people. But the metal ones still follow.

I charge through the single doorway into Heaven. They are everywhere outside, closing in. Not afraid to attack me inside the walls of Heaven. I close the door and as I bar it, I can hear metal claws scratching on the walls outside. I can hear clicking and shrieking.

"There are animals growing out of the Earth!" I tell Themroc, fury-petting the metal woman's head.

"Nothing but teeth and hair can grow from flesh," says Themroc.

"There are metal babies growing on trees like fruit. Hundreds of metal creatures tried to kill me. They are outside trying to get in as we speak."

"You are delusional, Themroc."

"You have eyes of your own. Are they delusional as well?" pointing at the doorway, scratchy metal noises outside.

"I do not need proof to know that you are lying."

Themroc walks away.

I turn to another Themroc sitting on the ground staring into marbles...

*Me:* Themroc, please let me show you. They want to attack us.

*Themroc:* Everything here wants us dead. This is nothing new.

*Me:* So you believe me?

Themroc nods.
*Me:* We are in danger!
*Themroc:* We are safe.

"The metal people are the children of Earth," a smaller Themroc tells me. I have not seen this Themroc before. He looks like Themroc, but he is half the size. And his texture is like that of a ghost's. "They were given souls by nature as the humans were given souls by God."

*Me:* And did God give the Earth a soul?

*Small Themroc:* The Earth has a complicated soul. It is deep under the ground. It is not as old as a Themroc soul, but the most complex soul God created.

*Me:* Themroc souls are not complex?

*Small Themroc:* Themroc souls are the most precise and easy souls God could make. Our emotions are quite easy to understand and control.

*Me:* What about animals? Birds, fish, insects, dogs? They surely could not have more complicated souls than Themroc.

*Small Themroc:* Animals do not have souls. They were created by the earth to provide food for humans. Once the Earth developed a meat brain, it grew intelligence enough to create animals with souls. Such as the metal people.

*Me:* Are there any animals left?

*Small Themroc:* The Earth devoured all creatures without souls before it devoured the humans. Themrocs were in charge of this as well. Anything left living on the landscape these days has a soul.

*Me:* Do you ever wonder why I ask these questions that I, as a Themroc, should already know?

*Small Themroc:* You have been away for a long time, Themroc. It is understandable for Themrocs to forget.

He hands me some marbles.

*Small Themroc:* You look almost sad, Themroc. You are quite skilled at impersonating that emotion. God is usually the only other person who makes that face around here.

*Me:* Yes, God is very sad...

*Small Themroc:* Oh, but there are the people in the basement who also make that face. They can make a sad face much better than you. Almost as good as God.

*Me:* Are they humans?

*Small Themroc:* There's a whole colony of them down there. Very interesting ones. And God doesn't know about them. We've been hiding them from Him. For hundreds of years we've been plucking our favorite souls from the world and hiding them in our basement. But they must not like the basement, because they are so very sad.

*Me:* Can I see them?

*Small Themroc:* Only the night serpent can take you into the basement.

*Me:* Where is the night serpent?

*Small Themroc:* He only comes out when the sky is red.

*Me:* There are no windows here. I can never tell when the sky is red. And I won't dare open the door to all the animals trying to get inside.

*Small Themroc:* All the clocks in Heaven change color with the color of the sky.

I look to a clock on a large nude sculpture. The face of the clock has a slight tint of green.

*Me:* So when it turns red I can see the night serpent?

*Small Themroc:* I'll have him sent to your room.

I spend the rest of the day waiting for a clock to turn red.

My neck cricks with excitement as I think of the people in the basement. Themroc is no company to me at all. They are so bland and inhuman. Even less human than my metal woman.

I need human contact. I need to get the people out of the basement and start a new society somewhere.

Thinking: Right now I am standing above people such as Beethoven, Einstein, Aristotle, Mark Twain! I can create a society of human legends. And I will be so loved by them, their savior. And the world we create for our children will be the greatest civilization to walk the Earth!

I twist my fingers and my toes together. I smile until my lips hurt. I touch my nose to my knees and then rub it back and forth until flakes of skin fall to the floor...

# CHAPTER THIRTEEN

It has been days, maybe, since I've slept. I refuse to sleep until I free the people in the basement. They are all sad down there and only I can make them happy. But the clock is so stubborn. It stays green all the time.

I can hear metal claws outside, climbing like spiders and waiting for a chance to get inside. I am so weak right now from lack of sleep that I won't be able to resist death if they get through. I would open up my arms and fall asleep into their razor claws.

The clock is still green, but I cannot wait for red any longer. My eyelids curling up over the crusty balls, dehydration in my flesh.

It will be red time when I wake up and the night serpent will take me to a new civilization.

Waking to the morning dog at my feet staring up my blankets and wagging its baby-arm tail.

I check the clock and it is still green-tinted.

"No, morning dog, I did not want to wake for anyone but the night serpent."

The morning dog is excited at hearing words come out of my mouth and starts bouncing up and down, jiggling his plump.

"I am so tired. Please let me sleep."

The morning dog gets even more excited at my continuation of speech, leaping onto my bed and jumping off, then back on the bed and then down to the floor.

"The night serpent will take me to a new life where I will be happy. I am expecting him at any minute."

The morning dog races in circles, knocking over bedroom decorations and plants.

I realize all he wants is a good petting and afterwards he will leave me alone. But as I go to pat him on the head, the dog collapses in exhaustion. I pet his sweaty neck with the back of my hand and now my obligation to him is over.

Before going back into sleep I realize the morning dog is too tired to leave. He is panting heavily, heat pouring out of its chest.

I try to pull him by the collar, but he still won't stand. I try making a tiny walker for the dog, but nothing is good enough. He is on the ground for good.

His face is still happy in my presence, looks as if he is smiling. I go to the bathroom and he whines until I come back. He tries to move but hasn't the energy to get on his feet.

"Morning dog, you have to leave now. I don't want you in my room when the night serpent arrives."

I try to go back to sleep, but the smell of the morning dog keeps me awake.

I put on a robe and step into the hallway. The morning dog whines again.

"I'm going downstairs for ten minutes," I tell the morning dog. "I don't want to see you here when I get back."

Downstairs:

Themrocs are pacing in circles. They are not spending their time looking inside of blue marbles, too agitated to be entertained. Well, every few steps a Themroc will sneak a peak at one hiding under his sleeve, peering into it for only a few seconds and then putting it away with full disregard, not even telling anyone about what he's seen inside.

When I get down to them, I am about to ask what is going on.

*Themroc:* Have you seen the morning dog?

My face nervous-twists.

*Me:* He is lying in my bedroom.

The entire hall bursts with sighs after my words. They end their pacing and some of them leave to go back to work.

The curious Themrocs stay.

*Themroc:* Why is he in your room?

*Themroc:* What happened to him?

*Themroc:* He hasn't been to my bedroom today.

*Themroc:* Is he alright?

*Themroc:* Is the world over?

*Me:* I awoke to the morning dog at my bedside. I don't know what he was doing there.

*Themroc:* You are supposed to be awake when the morning dog comes to your room.

*Themroc:* You have delayed the change from greentime to redtime.

*Me:* I don't understand the importance of the morning dog.

The curious Themrocs are now angry Themrocs.

*Themroc:* Without the morning dog, the world will end.

*Me:* Who tells you this?

*Themroc:* God tells us this.

*Me:* I cannot find the logic in this.

*Themroc:* God is the creator of logic. Only He knows what is logical and what is not.

*Me:* But what is the significance of petting a dog?

*Themroc:* It is like the click of a clock. Time depends on us to make it move.

*Themroc:* Without Themrocs or the morning dog, nothing can go into the future.

*Themroc:* Like the sun moving from city to city, is the morning dog walking from room to room.

*Themroc:* The comfort of the morning dog's company is like the comfort of the sun's rays.

*Me:* So is the night serpent like the moon?

*Themroc:* Who has spoken to you about the night serpent?

*Me:* Themroc has.

*Themroc:* You have been gone for quite some time, so we will not hold the comment against you. But the night serpent should not be discussed. He is all that is anti-Themroc in Heaven.

*Me:* Does he come to our rooms every day as the morning dog?

*Themroc:* He is not to be discussed.

I take Themrocs up the cloud-world stairs to my dark wet room to show them the morning dog lying near my bed, panting heavily with a big smile on its face. All Themrocs cry out, rushing to the morning dog, petting and comforting the miserable beast.

*Themroc:* What is wrong with him?

*Me:* He over-excited himself and collapsed with exhaustion.

*Themroc:* Oh, poor poor morning dog.

*Themroc:* You must have teased the morning dog. Your duty is to pet the morning dog not exhaust him.

*Me:* I did nothing to the morning dog. I was trying to sleep.

Themroc examines the morning dog, tries to help him up.

*Themroc:* The morning dog has lost feeling in his hind legs. He will never walk again.

Themrocs weep, crying out to the ceiling. Oh poor poor morning dog! Poor poor poor poor!

*Themroc:* He'll have to be put to sleep.

*Me:* He's just tired. He'll be okay soon.

*Themroc:* You've killed the morning dog!

*Themroc:* Oh, poor poor morning dog!

*Themroc:* The morning dog can no longer travel from bedroom to bedroom. The world will end tonight!

*Themroc:* You've killed the morning dog and you've ended the world!

*Themroc:* This is terrible!

*Themroc:* Poor morning dog!

*Themroc:* There is a metal woman's head on your pillow!

*Me:* I have not killed anything. The morning dog is still alive. If he's lost the use of his legs, we can just carry him from room to room.

*Themroc:* But he is in pain. We must do the merciful thing and end his misery.

I look at the morning dog smiling at us and wagging its baby arm/tail.

*Themroc:* Tonight the world will end. The night serpent will journey from room to room to collect us and remove us from this world forever.

*Me:* The night serpent is coming?

*Themroc:* Oh, how horrible it will be to see the night serpent. How horrible it will be to see it in our rooms rather than the adorable morning dog.

*Themroc:* Poor poor morning dog.

*Themroc:* You have ended our world.

The Themrocs lift the morning dog and carry it out of my bedroom, taking it downstairs to be killed.

"The world isn't going to end," I tell them. "It's just about to begin again."

I am petting the metal woman's head. The decomposing flesh inside emits a rotten yet sweet odor. At first it made me sick-dizzy but I have grown to appreciate its delicate flavor. Her kisses are an acquired taste.

The clock is now tinted red. This is the first time I have ever been happy for redfall, happy greentime has passed.

There is chaos in Heaven. I can hear Themrocs busy preparing themselves for the end of the world. They scream in drab Themroc ways, emotionless clamor.

An hour passes and there is a knock at the door. Then enters a long snake coiled into the shape of a man and wearing a business suit.

*Me:* You are the night serpent?

*Night Serpent:* Yes.

His language is very human for a snake.

*Me:* So the world is really going to end?

*Night Serpent:* Only for Themrocs.

The snake looks at my name tag and then to my face.

*Night Serpent:* But you are not Themroc. You are human.

*Me:* Yes, I do not fit in with Themroc culture. I was hoping you could bring me to the basement to free the humans that are hidden there.

*Night Serpent:* I'll take you there, but they are not being held prisoner.

*Me:* Themroc has imprisoned them in the dungeon.

*Night Serpent:* No, they are free to go anytime they like. They just don't want to go. The outside world is much uglier than the basement.

*Me:* I'll have to convince them to leave. Can we go there now?

*Night Serpent:* Not yet. We must wait until the new hour.

I nod and look at the clock, sitting on the bed.

The night serpent stays in its place, gazing the room with its snake eyes and spindly tongue.

*Me:* So Themroc exaggerated. The world is not really going to end.

*Night Serpent:* Their world is going to end, but not yours.

*Me:* So you are going room to room to kill them?

*Night Serpent:* No. I am here to collect their souls. I am like the Grim Reaper to Themrocs. The metal ones are here to kill them. They have just broken through the doorway to Heaven. They want to destroy this place and all of its inhabitants.

*Me:* It is my fault the metal people are angry.

*Night Serpent:* No, it is not your fault.
*Me:* Then why are the metal people trying to kill us?
*Night Serpent:* They are angry at God.
*Me:* What has God done?
*Night Serpent:* God ended all the interesting things.

I take the metal woman's head with me. I can't leave her behind. She is my love. My nose has grown attached to her decay-sweet scent. We must stay together forever, as a man is supposed to do with his wife.

The night serpent uncoils out of human form and reveals angel wings on its back, like a dragon without legs. I climb on his back and he carries me up and away. Over the main floor of Heaven.

I see an army of metal people below, like hundreds of soldier crabs. Themrocs are fighting them with silverware and pieces of furniture, but the metal claws are too much for them. Several Themrocs fall and their flesh is torn from their body in spaghetti strips. White blood-like fluid sprays out of the Themrocs, coating the metal people's armor.

We go up a chimney and through twisty passages until I can't see anymore. After several turns, we arrive in a small room lit by only a single candle.

*Night Serpent:* These are my quarters. Under your feet there is a trapdoor that leads down into the basement. You will find the surviving members of your race living there.

*Me:* Will the metal people get to me here?

*Night Serpent:* Don't worry. You are safe from them. Go now. My skills are required elsewhere.

*Me:* Sorry...

I get ready to open the metal trap door, underneath a muddy red carpet, but my hands stop me.

*Night Serpent:* What is wrong?

*Me:* I guess I'm nervous. What if they really don't want to go with me to start a new society?

*Night Serpent:* They won't. They already have a society down there and it is better than anything you could start on the surface of this world.

*Me:* It's really not a horrible place?

*Night Serpent:* All the greatest and most interesting products of the human race have built their own society down there. Now you can live among them.

*Me:* But I am not great or interesting. I don't think I'll fit in.

*Night Serpent:* You are not the type to normally fit in. Because of this, you will fit in. See, all of these people were considered strange in their time. They were all too unique and individual to fit in. Outcasts, all of them. This made them special and interesting. Their individuality is the reason the Themrocs kept them alive for all this time. You'll do just fine.

And the night serpent flies away, whooshing out the candle flame with its wind-flapping wings.

# CHAPTER FOURTEEN

I am sitting at a bus stop, angry with the steam-powered tram-truck that is always late to give me a lift back to my apartment. The corndog in my stomach is not digesting well. My nerves are irritated, extra sensitive, and my underwear is scratching up the inside of my thighs...

Sighing. I look down at the metal woman's head in my lap. My nose goes to the neck and sniffs hard, but the sweet rot-smell has faded. Her flesh under the metal has dehydrated away. Sometimes dust crumbles out of her and onto my slacks. I usually have to brush the flakes away before entering any social situation.

A woman sits down next to me on the bench, ogling me with an awkward yet piercing look. Her clothes are masculine, jeans and a muscle shirt. Thin tight muscles laced with tattoos.

"I like your head," the woman says to me, twisting her fingers.

She has to point to my lap to get me to understand.

"Oh yes," I say. "It is my ex-wife's head."

"She must have been beautiful."

"Yes... "

We look away from each other. I see her trying to catch my eyes. I am like a painting to her.

"I'm Kathy," says the woman.

I nod at her and pet my metal woman's head.

She blinks and then taps her fingernails on the metal woman's forehead. Her eyes scramble the cityscape.

*Kathy:* So they don't scare you either?

*Me:* Who?

*Kathy:* The Ongliers.

*Me:* I've never heard of them.

*Kathy:* Wiry creatures who live in the shadows. They attack anyone they find walking alone in the streets.

*Me:* We are immortal. They can't kill us. Why would we be afraid?

*Kathy:* They dismember you and rip you into bits. Yeah, you won't die. But you'll have to live forever as little pieces.

*Me:* But they only kill people that are alone?

*Kathy:* That's what they say. Only loners, like us.

*Me:* I can't handle being a loner.

*Kathy:* They've had many victims.

Her lips flare as if the thought excites her.

*Me:* How many?

*Kathy:* The majority of us are gone now. About seventy percent of the original citizens are now in bits and pieces all over the city. In gutters. In sidewalk cracks. But they are still alive.

*Me:* And you're not scared of being alone?

*Kathy:* I believe that getting ripped into pieces can be erotic.

I hide my metal woman's eyes from Kathy.

*Me:* I've been living alone in my apartment. Can they get me when I sleep?

*Kathy:* They can get you anywhere when you're alone.

*Me:* What am I going to do?

*Kathy:* You're going to move in with me.

*Me:* I don't know you. It'll be awkward.

*Kathy:* I prefer to live with strangers. It's more interesting.

*Me:* I guess I'd rather not be alone...

*Kathy:* Want to come home with me now?

*Me:* Sure.

She stands and walks away from me.

*Me:* Where are you going?

*Kathy:* Home. Come on.
*Me:* Don't you ride the tram-truck?
*Kathy:* No. I live right there. The third floor.
*Me:* Is it okay if I bring my wife's head?
*Kathy:* Hurry up. I made us dinner.
*Me:* Dinner?
*Kathy:* Do you like spaghetti? It's on the table getting cold.

*Kathy:* What was it like?
*Me:* What?
*Kathy:* Your metal wife. What was the sex like?
*Me:* Awkward. Painful sometimes.
*Kathy:* Were her nails metal too?
*Me:* She had claws like razor.
Kathy smiles with the side of her lips and blushes.
*Kathy:* There's only the one bed.
*Me:* You mentioned that earlier.
*Kathy:* We should go to sleep soon. Ongliers never attack sleeping couples.
*Me:* When are the performances?
*Kathy:* What performances?
*Me:* There is a list of performances on the board outside of the theater. I wrote down all the dates and times, but every time I go to a show I am the only one there.
Kathy laughs and clanks her fork on her plate.
*Kathy:* There hasn't been a play in years.
I look down at the spaghetti leftovers, all the bland pieces, and fight a rusty black dot on the side of my brain.
*Me:* What does everyone do for fun then?
*Kathy:* Everyone tries everything at least once. We exist from day to day so that we can amuse ourselves or each other. We have sex a lot. We play games. We write and paint. We're rarely ever bored.

*Me:* I have not had much fun since I've been here. I don't seem to fit in.

*Kathy:* Oh, you need friends. I'll help you fit in.

*Me:* I don't know. I can't relate to anyone. I can't be like everyone else.

*Kathy:* That's your problem. You try to be like everyone else. Everyone is unique here. They won't like you unless you be your own person.

*Me:* I don't like their attitude. Everyone should be the same. How else can we relate to each other?

*Kathy:* You're funny! Okay, you can be like me then.

*Me:* How do I be like you?

*Kathy:* For starters you can cut your dick off.

She laughs at me. I frown at her.

*Kathy:* You can be more experimental in life, in bed.

*Me:* Being experimental would help me fit in?

*Kathy:* It couldn't hurt.

*Me:* I guess it couldn't.

*Kathy:* Do you like tattoos?

I shrug.

*Kathy:* We need to get you some tattoos.

At the window, while Kathy is slicing clothes off of her body with a straight razor, I see some white claws in the street disassembling a dead animal. No... an old man. Lying there in the street as his flesh and bones are minced into piles around him. I don't see the creatures attacking him. They are covered in shadows and their movements are water-smooth and fast, whirlpool.

Kathy is in the bed of sewn together clothing, staring at my reflection in the window. Her face is blank, thinking of something else. Perhaps angry at me.

*Me:* Is there any place safe in the world?

*Kathy:* Even places in your mind are not safe.

Her belly flattens on the mattress and she reaches out to me, tickles me with a nail through a hole in my shirt.

There is a breakfast table in the middle of the street, in the center of a major intersection downtown. But there are no cars or people around. Just Kathy and I. Hushed. Pieces of human skin blowing in the dark cellar winds like autumn leaves.

The scene is lonely. A few windows are lighted in the surrounding buildings, but I see no people inside them.

The breakfast table is covered in a white cloth and cluttered with silver dishes and fruit baskets. Kathy sits me down at one side of the table and seats herself across from me. Now we can look at each other and maybe smile or wink during breakfast.

I do not carry around my metal woman's head anymore. I perched it on the windowsill at Kathy's apartment so it can look out at the beautiful civilization. It breaks the metal woman's head's heart to see me with Kathy. The head is just an ornament to me now, a memento of my dead wife, and I do not kiss it or sleep with it anymore. I'm with Kathy now.

Most of the breakfast food is dried out fruit and bread that tastes like it was put out here a day or two ago. I have had very little bread in my lifetime, but I can tell stale bread from fresh bread. This is very stale. I've never met anyone who thinks that stale bread tastes good enough to eat, so I do not eat it. I am very hungry to eat it, but the bread disgusts me.

The table is set for eight people but only two others arrive.

Kathy introduces them as Georges and Sylvia.

*Georges:* It isn't proper to speak on Tuesdays. And on Wednesdays, it isn't proper to listen. It isn't a good idea to enjoy smells or tastes on Thursdays. As for Fridays, you better not look in mirrors. On Saturdays, don't touch a thing! And on Sundays, whatever you do, do not even think about thinking. To think on a Sunday is death to one's social life.

*Sylvia:* What about Mondays?

Georges raises an eyebrow. "Mondays you don't ask questions."

*Sylvia to Kathy:* Is it Monday then?

Kathy nods and they break into snickers.

I write all of Georges' rules on my napkin, trying to absorb them into my memory as quickly as possible.

*Me:* Tell me all the rules there are. I am new here and plan on following all of the social rules devotedly.

Sylvia smiles at Georges who clears his throat and straightens his bow tie. His voice is deeper when he explains things.

*Georges:* All rules apply on a specific day of the week, except on holidays when you are not allowed to work, rest, or have any fun. On the last day of every month, it is very sociable to go without eating or sleeping... unless it is the last day of February during a leap year. In this case, it is okay to eat but completely unacceptable to breathe.

Sylvia is cackling now.

*Kathy to me:* Don't mind them. They are drunk and just having fun with you.

*Georges:* Forgive me, young man. Eternity makes things so tiresome sometimes. These days I have to resort to liquor in order to amuse myself. It's a shame that in a few years all of its pleasantries will wear off. I'll have to wait at least two decades before it becomes desirable again.

*Sylvia:* Exploring the mind is more exciting than anything liquor can do for us.

*Kathy:* Or exploring the flesh.

Georges smiles at the ladies.

*Georges:* But my mind is old. My flesh is old. I am immortal, but I am weak and tired. I don't have the physical and mental energy that you do. I'm just an old man who can't die of old age.

*Sylvia:* Oh, please, you're not that old. There are dozens of people at least thirty years older than you and twice as withered. But I don't see them bitching and complaining about their age like you do.

*Georges:* They don't bitch because they are in pieces right now. I'm the only old guy left who hasn't been chopped into bits.

*Sylvia:* Yet...

Georges waves her words away.

*Georges to Kathy:* So what are your plans for the day?

*Kathy:* I'm thinking about taking the new guy on my usual tour.

*Sylvia:* Oh, how exciting! Can I join you?

*Kathy:* Not this time, but perhaps soon. I want to make him last. He's the very last addition to our community.

*Sylvia:* The last? And why's that?

*Me:* All the other humans in the world are dead.

*Sylvia:* Is that so...

*Me:* The people in this town are all that's left of the human race.

*Georges:* How depressing...

*Kathy:* I think being one of the last humans alive is fascinating. Even romantic.

*Me:* I like being here. It's been a while since I've had any human contact. The world is very lonely outside the cellar. It is paradise here compared to where I'm from.

*Sylvia:* What has become of the world since we've left?

I look down at a filmy grapefruit.

*Kathy:* He doesn't like to talk about it during a meal or before sex.

*Me:* The only way to describe the Earth these days is to compare it to rotten food or rotten sex.

*Georges:* It doesn't sound like it's changed much.

*Sylvia:* Nothing ever changes.

*Kathy:* Everything changes. You've just forgotten how to see change. You're blind to it.

*Me:* No one was blind when the Earth changed.

*Sylvia:* Someone had to be blind. Someone is always blind.

# CHAPTER FIFTEEN

Kathy wants to give me a tour of the city today. It is very interesting to learn the history of the community. Their culture started as a handful of people trapped in Heaven's large shadowy basement. It was a crude lifestyle at first, but they learned how to grow, to create a whole town in the darkness. There was even a time when Themrocs would visit and help with the building of the society. The Themrocs treated the people like dogs/cats, or maybe like ants in an ant farm.

Every once in a while, Kathy will pull me into a corner or into a wishing fountain or onto a town monument and she'll make vicious love to me. She'll dig her nails into my back and wrap her legs around me. I think her tour is just a mask. I think she is just trying to trick me into certain locations of the town that are sexually exciting to her. I bet she's been tricking/molesting newcomers for ages. Sylvia seemed familiar with her plan. I'm sure Kathy is well-known for her games.

We become tired after fucking in the lighthouse. There were a couple silent men up there, but they pretended not to notice us.

"The lighthouse is always occupied," Kathy tells me, winking. "It holds up our sun. Without the light house we would be in total darkness."

*Me:* That was an exciting day.

*Kathy:* Yes, you make things exciting.

*Me:* I am not an exciting person.

*Kathy:* But you are new. New is always exciting. The way I normally keep from getting bored is by looking at old things like they are new things.

*Me:* Themrocs used to look at marbles all the time.

*Kathy:* For entertainment?

*Me:* They keep the souls of humans inside of marbles. For entertainment, they would look into marbles and watch the story of that person's life inside.

*Kathy:* Like a movie?

*Me:* I'm not really sure what they were like. I could never see anything in the marbles.

*Kathy:* I wish we had some of those. How many marbles did they have?

*Me:* Billions, probably. Nobody ever counted them.

*Kathy:* Those marbles could entertain us for centuries. Can we get some?

*Me:* We'd have to leave the town. I'm not sure what we'll find outside of here. The house of Themroc was being destroyed as I was leaving it. I escaped death to come here.

Eyes lighting up...

*Kathy:* It's worth the risk. All those stories...

*Me:* We can try. But it might not be possible.

*Kathy:* Do the souls in the marbles sense what is around them? Will they know if I am holding them?

*Me:* I don't know.

*Kathy:* If I put one into my cunt will it feel the insides of me?

*Me:* Themrocs weren't at all sexual with them.

*Kathy:* I used to find pieces of people after they were chopped up by Ongliers and masturbate with them. The pieces were still alive and warm. They would wiggle when I'd rub them against my clit. I'm not sure, but I like to believe that the person who used to own that part of flesh could feel the insides of me. The thought made me so horny.

I try not to listen anymore. My attention is outside of the window, staring over the metal woman's head and watching for Ongliers.

*Kathy:* Sometimes I would even swallow the flesh pieces while I was masturbating. Thinking about pieces of people dissolving in my belly gave me wild orgasms. I bet they have become a part of me and are living through me somehow. I wonder if they can see what I see...

In the reflection of the window, I can see Kathy licking her lips and caressing her body parts as if they are someone else's.

We do not go back to the surface for some time. Kathy not at all impatient to go.

*Kathy:* All the time in the world lives in this town.

So Kathy spends a few weeks exploring me, brain and body. She finds things in me that I've never found and brings them out of me to show her friends.

Kathy is not all about sex. She talks a lot about sex and has lots of sex, but she is more interested in exploring people and behaviors. She is the most intelligent and interesting person I've met. She says I am also interesting and promises to prove it to me someday. I don't know how she can say I'm interesting. Perhaps because I am so new. I am like a blank piece of paper to her. A story waiting to happen.

On odd days, Kathy has me eating chili peppers from the wet parts of her body. She says the burn is erotic. My lips are on fire and when she kisses me her tongue feels like lava in my mouth. She says it takes a while to get used to the peppers. Once I do I'll be able to taste the chili flavor and the burning sensation will make me feel alive.

Kathy is always interested in things that make her feel alive.

On even days, Kathy makes me call her Stephen and she'll dress up in masculine clothing. She still looks beautiful to me. I believe that I think she is beautiful normally. I'm not sure if I find her beautiful or just sexy. Or maybe I am in love with her. I believe I might be in love with her. She tells me to tell her I

71

love her when she is dressed up like Stephen. And I always tell her things she tells me to tell her...

Kathy's Stephen outfits are not much different than her Kathy outfits. She always dresses a little masculine. But her Stephen attitude is not similar to her Kathy attitude. Stephen is much more demanding/controlling, likes everything his way. Kathy is more interesting and easygoing and always coming up with fun things to do.

Today is an even day, so Kathy has turned into Stephen and makes me call her Stephen. On even mornings, I always call her Kathy until she corrects me, hoping that someday she won't be in the mood to be a man.

*Stephen:* Look into my eyes when you're talking to me.

*Me:* I'm not saying anything.

*Stephen:* Then say something to me.

I can never think of anything to say when Stephen does this to me.

*Me:* It's time to collect marbles on the surface.

*Stephen:* Go tomorrow.

*Me:* Why not today?

*Stephen:* Because I don't want to go anywhere. Go with Kathy tomorrow.

Outside there is a crowd of people staggering through the streets with lowered heads and hands in their pockets. Their footsteps are slow and sound like squeaky rocking chairs.

*Me:* Where are they going?

*Stephen:* Some of the children must have been molesting each other in an ally somewhere. The children will do this on occasion and if someone mature catches them in the act, all of the townspeople go into mourning and walk aimlessly through the streets for the rest of the day. It is very hard on the children who will never grow old enough to have socially acceptable sex. And it is very hard on the adults to witness young children engaging in sexual activity.

*Me:* I wouldn't think that children have a sexual drive at all.

*Stephen:* Humans are born a with sexual drive.

It would be best to never see children having sex. But children that are hundreds of years older than me will do what they want to do. They don't even care if I see. They don't even care that they upset and disturb the whole town.

*Stephen:* The sexual experiences of childhood, no matter how slight and subtle, are what create the several fetishes we crave as adults.

*Me:* I was not sexually active as a child.

*Stephen:* Everything is sexual to a child. You just didn't know what sex was at the time.

*Me:* I don't remember being a child at all.

*Stephen:* It's good to have poor memory. For you, old things become new things very easily.

# CHAPTER SIXTEEN

Kathy and I leave town in the morning when it is red-vibrating.

We open the black iron door to the cellar of Heaven. We do not need the night serpent to do this. I warned Kathy that we might not be able to leave the cellar without the night serpent's assistance. She just smiles my wrinkled attitude away.

Beyond the town, we find ourselves out in the fresh lime-flavored greentime air. The night serpent's lair is open to sky, and Heaven has been collapsed into piles of rubble around us.

*Kathy:* The ground isn't meat like you said.

*Me:* We aren't on the ground yet. It is all meat outside of Heaven.

*Kathy:* I want to see.

I lead Kathy to the top of a rubble hill and show her the landscape.

Kathy's glistening eyes go razor wire, fists squeezing tight, when she sees the flesh world.

*Kathy:* The whole world is like this now?

I nod.

*Kathy:* And you lived here.

*Me:* This is the Earth I've always known.

Kathy is in love with the flesh ground. She runs down the garbage heap and embraces the Earth. Rubs her body against it. Licks and bites it.

*Kathy:* Come down here to me.

Pulling off her clothes.

*Me:* Give me a few minutes.

Something is in the air. A smell of dead angels.

God is dead. Or maybe He ran away after the metal people tore Heaven to the ground.

Maybe He killed Himself after the night serpent took all

the Themrocs away from Heaven, leaving Him completely/ utterly alone. Or maybe the metal people killed Him before He got the chance.

He could still be alive somewhere. He could have left Heaven to be a normal man, to live like a hermit on the teeth and tongue landscape. Maybe He moved into the windmill with the oldman/child, the Themroc who was the most human. Maybe they converse to each other, dine together, plow the herpes fields together, make puppet shows for each other. An ex-angel and an ex-God, retiring into the country...

I find a couple of marbles in the rubble. They were squeezed tight into a Themroc-corpse hand.

I show them to Kathy.

Her eyes pop with happy glimmers. She takes one and holds it near her vision. Eyes fade into a haze, like she is far away. She doesn't move for several minutes. Half of an hour. An hour.

When she is finished she shakes her head and begins to cry.

*Kathy:* It's beautiful.

And she holds herself and lets all the tears come out of her. She still seems far away.

I look into the same marble, but I see nothing but the inside of a marble.

We camp on top of the ruins, build a fire out of the wood scraps leftover from Heaven.

The city of demons is glowing blue in the distance. Jellyfish fill themselves with electricity, wandering the building tops, oozing trails of blue light. Turning everything alive again.

Kathy sleeps against me, dreaming about the billions of marbles she will collect in the months to come. I sleep and dream with her, but I don't have dreams about marbles.

I dream about an Earth far away from here. A fleshy world

that grows colorful forests and mountains, oceans that go from green to red each day. There are sailboats traveling from country to country, explorers or perhaps tradesmen. And the people in these ships are made of metal. They are at peace with the rest of the world.

From a distance, I watch them grow. I watch their societies flourish from primitive animalism to civilized intelligence. I see weddings and children and music and ceremonies and governments and funerals and celebrations and struggles and triumphs and many other beautiful things.

I awake to the red sky and watch it deeply, as if I am Kathy or Themroc looking into a marble.

I'm not sure where I will go from here. The world is a giant place, but it is no longer for me. I'll have to go back underground with Kathy and live there forever, sometimes coming out to peek at the progress of the metal people.

Maybe I'll be torn into bits and pieces by the monsters that hide in the shadows down there. Maybe Kathy will masturbate with my pieces and then swallow them, so that I will become a part of her.

Or perhaps I'll never be torn into bits. Perhaps I will live long enough to see the metal people evolve as far as humans did. Then I might even step out of the underground town and join their society. I can be a living history book for them. I can teach them things they do not know.

And if they don't have them already, I can introduce them to shopping malls and television commercials and forty-hour work weeks and churches and fancy dinner parties and art stores and corporate boy bands and football teams and blockbuster movies and social ladders and designer clothes and voting booths and bank accounts and fast food chains and all the other important things from the old world...

So that the metal people will be more human.

So that I will feel more at home.

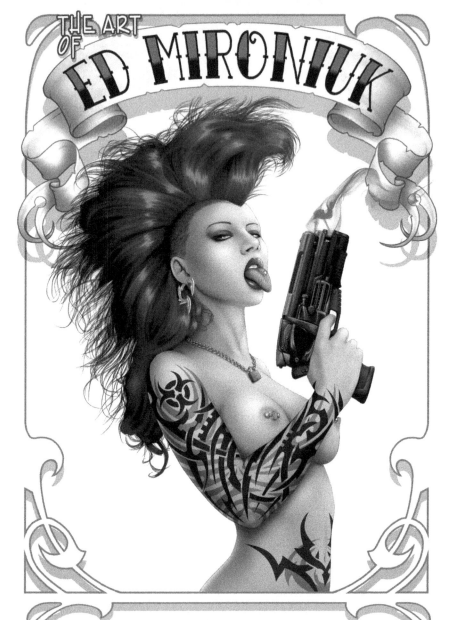

# THE ART OF ED MIRONIUK

**48 full color pages of kinky and kutie pin-up
girls with a rough and ready attitude
hand signed with original one of a kind sketch
$40**

**http://edmironiuk.bigcartel.com/**

"Fetish pinup girls that are as interesting and strange as they
are sexy. The more you see of Ed Mironiuk's art, the more it
will attach itself to you. This book is a must-buy."
*Carlton Mellick III*

## ABOUT THE AUTHOR

**Carlton Mellick III** is one of the leading authors of the bizarro fiction subgenre. Since 2001, his books have drawn an international cult following, despite the fact that they have been shunned by most libraries and chain bookstores.

He won the Wonderland Book Award for his novel, *Warrior Wolf Women of the Wasteland*, in 2009. His short fiction has appeared in *Vice Magazine, The Year's Best Fantasy and Horror #16, The Magazine of Bizarro Fiction,* and *Zombies: Encounters with the Hungry Dead*, among others. He is also a graduate of Clarion West, where he studied under the likes of Chuck Palahniuk, Connie Willis, and Cory Doctorow.

He lives in Portland, OR, the bizarro fiction mecca.

Visit him online at **www.carltonmellick.com**

# BIZARRO BOOKS

## CATALOG    SPRING 2012

**ERASERHEAD
PRESS**

Your major resource for the bizarro fiction genre:

# WWW.BIZARROCENTRAL.COM

Introduce yourselves to the bizarro fiction genre and all of its authors with the Bizarro Starter Kit series. Each volume features short novels and short stories by ten of the leading bizarro authors, designed to give you a perfect sampling of the genre for only $10.

### BB-0X1
### "The Bizarro Starter Kit" (Orange)
Featuring D. Harlan Wilson, Carlton Mellick III, Jeremy Robert Johnson, Kevin L Donihe, Gina Ranalli, Andre Duza, Vincent W. Sakowski, Steve Beard, John Edward Lawson, and Bruce Taylor. **236 pages   $10**

### BB-0X2
### "The Bizarro Starter Kit" (Blue)
Featuring Ray Fracalossy, Jeremy C. Shipp, Jordan Krall, Mykle Hansen, Andersen Prunty, Eckhard Gerdes, Bradley Sands, Steve Aylett, Christian TeBordo, and Tony Rauch. **244 pages   $10**

### BB-0X2
### "The Bizarro Starter Kit" (Purple)
Featuring Russell Edson, Athena Villaverde, David Agranoff, Matthew Revert, Andrew Goldfarb, Jeff Burk, Garrett Cook, Kris Saknussemm, Cody Goodfellow, and Cameron Pierce **264 pages $10**

BB-001 **"The Kafka Effekt" D. Harlan Wilson** — A collection of forty-four irreal short stories loosely written in the vein of Franz Kafka, with more than a pinch of William S. Burroughs sprinkled on top. **211 pages   $14**

BB-002 **"Satan Burger"   Carlton Mellick III** — The cult novel that put Carlton Mellick III on the map ... Six punks get jobs at a fast food restaurant owned by the devil in a  city violently overpopulated by surreal alien cultures. **236 pages   $14**

BB-003 **"Some Things Are Better Left Unplugged" Vincent Sakwoski** — Join The Man and his Nemesis, the obese tabby, for a nightmare roller coaster ride into this postmodern fantasy. **152 pages   $10**

BB-004 **"Shall We Gather At the Garden?" Kevin L Donihe** — Donihe's Debut novel.  Midgets take over the world, The Church of Lionel Richie vs. The Church of the Byrds, plant porn and more! **244 pages   $14**

BB-005 **"Razor Wire Pubic Hair" Carlton Mellick III** — A genderless humandildo is purchased by a razor dominatrix and brought into her nightmarish world of bizarre sex and mutilation. **176 pages   $11**

BB-006 **"Stranger on the Loose" D. Harlan Wilson** — The fiction of Wilson's 2nd collection is planted in the soil of normalcy, but what grows out of that soil is a dark, witty, otherworldly jungle... **228 pages   $14**

BB-007 **"The Baby Jesus Butt Plug" Carlton Mellick III** — Using clones of the Baby Jesus for anal sex will be the hip sex fetish of the future. **92 pages   $10**

BB-008 **"Fishyfleshed" Carlton Mellick III** — The world of the past is an illogical flatland lacking in dimension and color, a sick-scape of crispy squid people wandering the desert for no apparent reason. **260 pages   $14**

BB-009 **"Dead Bitch Army" Andre Duza** — Step into a world filled with racist teenagers, cannibals, 100 warped Uncle Sams, automobiles with razor-sharp teeth, living graffiti, and a pissed-off zombie bitch out for revenge. **344 pages $16**

BB-010 **"The Menstruating Mall" Carlton Mellick III** — "The Breakfast Club meets Chopping Mall as directed by David Lynch." - Brian Keene **212 pages $12**

BB-011 **"Angel Dust Apocalypse" Jeremy Robert Johnson** — Meth-heads, man-made monsters, and murderous Neo-Nazis. "Seriously amazing short stories..." - Chuck Palahniuk, author of Fight Club **184 pages $11**

BB-012 **"Ocean of Lard" Kevin L Donihe / Carlton Mellick III** — A parody of those old Choose Your Own Adventure kid's books about some very odd pirates sailing on a sea made of animal fat. **176 pages $12**

BB-015 **"Foop!" Chris Genoa** — Strange happenings are going on at Dactyl, Inc, the world's first and only time travel tourism company. "A surreal pie in the face!" - Christopher Moore **300 pages $14**

BB-020 **"Punk Land" Carlton Mellick III** — In the punk version of Heaven, the anarchist utopia is threatened by corporate fascism and only Goblin, Mortician's sperm, and a blue-mohawked female assassin named Shark Girl can stop them. **284 pages $15**

BB-027 **"Siren Promised" Jeremy Robert Johnson & Alan M Clark** — Nominated for the Bram Stoker Award. A potent mix of bad drugs, bad dreams, brutal bad guys, and surreal/incredible art by Alan M. Clark. **190 pages $13**

BB-031**"Sea of the Patchwork Cats" Carlton Mellick III** — A quiet dreamlike tale set in the ashes of the human race. For Mellick enthusiasts who also adore The Twilight Zone. **112 pages $10**

BB-032 **"Extinction Journals" Jeremy Robert Johnson** — An uncanny voyage across a newly nuclear America where one man must confront the problems associated with loneliness, insane dieties, radiation, love, and an ever-evolving cockroach suit with a mind of its own. **104 pages $10**

BB-037 **"The Haunted Vagina" Carlton Mellick III** — It's difficult to love a woman whose vagina is a gateway to the world of the dead. **132 pages $10**

BB-043 **"War Slut" Carlton Mellick III** — Part "1984," part "Waiting for Godot," and part action horror video game adaptation of John Carpenter's "The Thing." **116 pages $10**

BB-047 **"Sausagey Santa" Carlton Mellick III** — A bizarro Christmas tale featuring Santa as a piratey mutant with a body made of sausages. 124 pages $10

BB-048 **"Misadventures in a Thumbnail Universe" Vincent Sakowski** — Dive deep into the surreal and satirical realms of neo-classical Blender Fiction, filled with television shoes and flesh-filled skies. **120 pages $10**

BB-053 **"Ballad of a Slow Poisoner" Andrew Goldfarb** — Millford Mutterwurst sat down on a Tuesday to take his afternoon tea, and made the unpleasant discovery that his elbows were becoming flatter. **128 pages $10**

BB-055 **"Help! A Bear is Eating Me" Mykle Hansen** — The bizarro, heartwarming, magical tale of poor planning, hubris and severe blood loss... **150 pages $11**

BB-056 **"Piecemeal June" Jordan Krall** — A man falls in love with a living sex doll, but with love comes danger when her creator comes after her with crab-squid assassins. **90 pages $9**

BB-058 **"The Overwhelming Urge" Andersen Prunty** — A collection of bizarro tales by Andersen Prunty. **150 pages   $11**

BB-059 **"Adolf in Wonderland" Carlton Mellick III** — A dreamlike adventure that takes a young descendant of Adolf Hitler's design and sends him down the rabbit hole into a world of imperfection and disorder. **180 pages   $11**

BB-061 **"Ultra Fuckers" Carlton Mellick III** — Absurdist suburban horror about a couple who enter an upper middle class gated community but can't find their way out. **108 pages  $9**

BB-062 **"House of Houses" Kevin L. Donihe** — An odd man wants to marry his house. Unfortunately, all of the houses in the world collapse at the same time in the Great House Holocaust. Now he must travel to House Heaven to find his departed fiancee. **172 pages   $11**

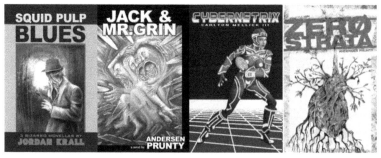

BB-064 **"Squid Pulp Blues" Jordan Krall** — In these three bizarro-noir novellas, the reader is thrown into a world of murderers, drugs made from squid parts, deformed gun-toting veterans, and a mischievous apocalyptic donkey. **204 pages $12**

BB-065 **"Jack and Mr. Grin" Andersen Prunty** — "When Mr. Grin calls you can hear a smile in his voice. Not a warm and friendly smile, but the kind that seizes your spine in fear. You don't need to pay your phone bill to hear it. That smile is in every line of Prunty's prose." - Tom Bradley. **208 pages  $12**

BB-066 **"Cybernetrix" Carlton Mellick III** — What would you do if your normal everyday world was slowly mutating into the video game world from Tron? **212 pages  $12**

BB-072 **"Zerostrata" Andersen Prunty** — Hansel Nothing lives in a tree house, suffers from memory loss, has a very eccentric family, and falls in love with a woman who runs naked through the woods every night. **144 pages  $11**

BB-073 **"The Egg Man" Carlton Mellick III** — It is a world where humans reproduce like insects. Children are the property of corporations, and having an enormous ten-foot brain implanted into your skull is a grotesque sexual fetish. Mellick's industrial urban dystopia is one of his darkest and grittiest to date. **184 pages $11**

BB-074 **"Shark Hunting in Paradise Garden" Cameron Pierce** — A group of strange humanoid religious fanatics travel back in time to the Garden of Eden to discover it is invested with hundreds of giant flying maneating sharks. **150 pages $10**

BB-075 **"Apeshit" Carlton Mellick III** - Friday the 13th meets Visitor Q. Six hipster teens go to a cabin in the woods inhabited by a deformed killer. An incredibly fucked-up parody of B-horror movies with a bizarro slant. **192 pages $12**

BB-076 **"Fuckers of Everything on the Crazy Shitting Planet of the Vomit At smosphere" Mykle Hansen** - Three bizarro satires. Monster Cocks, Journey to the Center of Agnes Cuddlebottom, and Crazy Shitting Planet. **228 pages $12**

BB-077 **"The Kissing Bug" Daniel Scott Buck** — In the tradition of Roald Dahl, Tim Burton, and Edward Gorey, comes this bizarro anti-war children's story about a bohemian conenose kissing bug who falls in love with a human woman. **116 pages $10**

BB-078 **"MachoPoni" Lotus Rose** — It's My Little Pony... *Bizarro* style! A long time ago Poniworld was split in two. On one side of the Jagged Line is the Pastel Kingdom, a magical land of music, parties, and positivity. On the other side of the Jagged Line is Dark Kingdom inhabited by an army of undead ponies. **148 pages $11**

BB-079 **"The Faggiest Vampire" Carlton Mellick III** — A Roald Dahl-esque children's story about two faggy vampires who partake in a mustache competition to find out which one is truly the faggiest. **104 pages $10**

BB-080 **"Sky Tongues" Gina Ranalli** — The autobiography of Sky Tongues, the biracial hermaphrodite actress with tongues for fingers. Follow her strange life story as she rises from freak to fame. **204 pages $12**

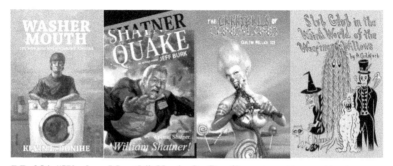

BB-081 **"Washer Mouth" Kevin L. Donihe** - A washing machine becomes human and pursues his dream of meeting his favorite soap opera star. **244 pages $11**

BB-082 **"Shatnerquake" Jeff Burk** - All of the characters ever played by William Shatner are suddenly sucked into our world. Their mission: hunt down and destroy the real William Shatner. **100 pages $10**

BB-083 **"The Cannibals of Candyland" Carlton Mellick III** - There exists a race of cannibals that are made of candy. They live in an underground world made out of candy. One man has dedicated his life to killing them all. **170 pages $11**

BB-084 **"Slub Glub in the Weird World of the Weeping Willows"** **Andrew Goldfarb** - The charming tale of a blue glob named Slub Glub who helps the weeping willows whose tears are flooding the earth. There are also hyenas, ghosts, and a voodoo priest **100 pages $10**

BB-085 **"Super Fetus" Adam Pepper** - Try to abort this fetus and he'll kick your ass! **104 pages $10**

BB-086 **"Fistful of Feet" Jordan Krall** - A bizarro tribute to spaghetti westerns, featuring Cthulhu-worshipping Indians, a woman with four feet, a crazed gunman who is obsessed with sucking on candy, Syphilis-ridden mutants, sexually transmitted tattoos, and a house devoted to the freakiest fetishes. **228 pages $12**

BB-087 **"Ass Goblins of Auschwitz" Cameron Pierce** - It's Monty Python meets Nazi exploitation in a surreal nightmare as can only be imagined by Bizarro author Cameron Pierce. **104 pages $10**

BB-088 **"Silent Weapons for Quiet Wars" Cody Goodfellow** - "This is high-end psychological surrealist horror meets bottom-feeding low-life crime in a techno-thrilling science fiction world full of Lovecraft and magic..." -John Skipp **212 pages $12**

### BB-089 "Warrior Wolf Women of the Wasteland" Carlton Mellick III
— Road Warrior Werewolves versus McDonaldland Mutants...post-apocalyptic fiction has never been quite like this. **316 pages $13**

### BB-091 "Super Giant Monster Time" Jeff Burk — A tribute to choose your own adventures and Godzilla movies. Will you escape the giant monsters that are rampaging the fuck out of your city and shit? Or will you join the mob of alien-controlled punk rockers causing chaos in the streets? What happens next depends on you. **188 pages $12**

### BB-092 "Perfect Union" Cody Goodfellow — "Cronenberg's THE FLY on a grand scale: human/insect gene-spliced body horror, where the human hive politics are as shocking as the gore." -John Skipp. **272 pages $13**

### BB-093 "Sunset with a Beard" Carlton Mellick III — 14 stories of surreal science fiction. **200 pages $12**

### BB-094 "My Fake War" Andersen Prunty — The absurd tale of an unlikely soldier forced to fight a war that, quite possibly, does not exist. It's Rambo meets Waiting for Godot in this subversive satire of American values and the scope of the human imagination. **128 pages $11**

### BB-095 "Lost in Cat Brain Land" Cameron Pierce — Sad stories from a surreal world. A fascist mustache, the ghost of Franz Kafka, a desert inside a dead cat. Primordial entities mourn the death of their child. The desperate serve tea to mysterious creatures. A hopeless romantic falls in love with a pterodactyl. And much more. **152 pages $11**

### BB-096 "The Kobold Wizard's Dildo of Enlightenment +2" Carlton Mellick III — A Dungeons and Dragons parody about a group of people who learn they are only made up characters in an AD&D campaign and must find a way to resist their nerdy teenaged players and retarded dungeon master in order to survive. **232 pages $12**

### BB-098 "A Hundred Horrible Sorrows of Ogner Stump" Andrew Goldfarb — Goldfarb's acclaimed comic series. A magical and weird journey into the horrors of everyday life. **164 pages $11**

### BB-099 "Pickled Apocalypse of Pancake Island" Cameron Pierce—A
demented fairy tale about a pickle, a pancake, and the apocalypse. **102 pages  $8**

### BB-100 "Slag Attack" Andersen Prunty— Slag Attack features four visceral,
noir stories about the living, crawling apocalypse.A slag is what survivors are calling the
slug-like maggots raining from the sky, burrowing inside people, and hollowing out their
flesh and their sanity. **148 pages   $11**

### BB-101 "Slaughterhouse High" Robert Devereaux—A place where
schools are built with secret passageways, rebellious teens get zippers installed in their
mouths and genitals, and once a year, on that special night, one couple is slaughtered and
the bits of their bodies are kept as souvenirs. **304 pages   $13**

### BB-102 "The Emerald Burrito of Oz" John Skipp & Marc Levinthal
—OZ IS REAL! Magic is real! The gate is really in Kansas! And America is finally allowing
Earth tourists to visit this weird-ass, mysterious land. But when Gene of Los Angeles heads off
for summer vacation in the Emerald City, little does he know that a war is brewing...a war that
could destroy both worlds. **280 pages $13**

### BB-103 "The Vegan Revolution... with Zombies" David Agranoff —
When there's no more meat in hell, the vegans will walk the earth. **160 pages   $11**

### BB-104 "The Flappy Parts" Kevin L Donihe—Poems about bunnies, LSD,
and police abuse. You know, things that matter. 132 **pages   $11**

### BB-105 "Sorry I Ruined Your Orgy" Bradley Sands—Bizarro humorist
Bradley Sands returns with one of the strangest, most hilarious collections of the year. **130
pages  $11**

### BB-106 "Mr. Magic Realism" Bruce Taylor—Like Golden Age science fic-
tion comics written by Freud, *Mr. Magic Realism* is a strange, insightful adventure that
spans the furthest reaches of the galaxy, exploring the hidden caverns in the hearts and
minds of men, women, aliens, and biomechanical cats. **152 pages   $11**

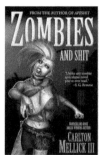   

BB-107 **"Zombies and Shit" Carlton Mellick III**—"Battle Royale" meets "Return of the Living Dead." Mellick's bizarro tribute to the zombie genre. **308 pages $13**

BB-108 **"The Cannibal's Guide to Ethical Living" Mykle Hansen**— Over a five star French meal of fine wine, organic vegetables and human flesh, a lunatic delivers a witty, chilling, disturbingly sane argument in favor of eating the rich.. **184 pages $11**

BB-109 **"Starfish Girl" Athena Villaverde**—In a post-apocalyptic underwater dome society, a girl with a starfish growing from her head and an assassin with sea anenome hair are on the run from a gang of mutant fish men. **160 pages $11**

BB-110 **"Lick Your Neighbor" Chris Genoa**—Mutant ninjas, a talking whale, kung fu masters, maniacal pilgrims, and an alcoholic clown populate Chris Genoa's surreal, darkly comical and unnerving reimagining of the first Thanksgiving. **303 pages $13**

BB-111 **"Night of the Assholes" Kevin L. Donihe**—A plague of assholes is infecting the countryside. Normal everyday people are transforming into jerks, snobs, dicks, and douchebags. And they all have only one purpose: to make your life a living hell.. **192 pages $11**

BB-112 **"Jimmy Plush, Teddy Bear Detective" Garrett Cook**—Hardboiled cases of a private detective trapped within a teddy bear body. **180 pages $11**

BB-113 **"The Deadheart Shelters" Forrest Armstrong**—The hip hop lovechild of William Burroughs and Dali... **144 pages $11**

BB-114 **"Eyeballs Growing All Over Me... Again" Tony Raugh**— Absurd, surreal, playful, dream-like, whimsical, and a lot of fun to read. **144 pages $11**

BB-115 **"Whargoul" Dave Brockie** — From the killing grounds of Stalingrad to the death camps of the holocaust. From torture chambers in Iraq to race riots in the United States, the Whargoul was there, killing and raping. **244 pages $12**

BB-116 **"By the Time We Leave Here, We'll Be Friends" J. David Osborne** — A David Lynchian nightmare set in a Russian gulag, where its prisoners, guards, traitors, soldiers, lovers, and demons fight for survival and their own rapidly deteriorating humanity. **168 pages $11**

BB-117 **"Christmas on Crack" edited by Carlton Mellick III** — Perverted Christmas Tales for the whole family! . . . as long as every member of your family is over the age of 18. **168 pages $11**

BB-118 **"Crab Town" Carlton Mellick III** — Radiation fetishists, balloon people, mutant crabs, sail-bike road warriors, and a love affair between a woman and an H-Bomb. This is one mean asshole of a city. Welcome to Crab Town. **100 pages $8**

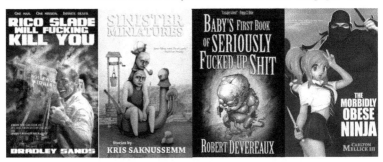

BB-119 **"Rico Slade Will Fucking Kill You" Bradley Sands** — Rico Slade is an action hero. Rico Slade can rip out a throat with his bare hands. Rico Slade's favorite food is the honey-roasted peanut. Rico Slade will fucking kill everyone. A novel. **122 pages $8**

BB-120 **"Sinister Miniatures" Kris Saknussemm** — The definitive collection of short fiction by Kris Saknussemm, confirming that he is one of the best, most daring writers of the weird to emerge in the twenty-first century. **180 pages $11**

BB-121 **"Baby's First Book of Seriously Fucked up Shit" Robert Devereaux** — Ten stories of the strange, the gross, and the just plain fucked up from one of the most original voices in horror. **176 pages $11**

BB-122 **"The Morbidly Obese Ninja" Carlton Mellick III** — These days, if you want to run a successful company . . . you're going to need a lot of ninjas. **92 pages $8**

BB-123 **"Abortion Arcade" Cameron Pierce** — An intoxicating blend of body horror and midnight movie madness, reminiscent of early David Lynch and the splatterpunks at their most sublime. **172 pages $11**

BB-124 **"Black Hole Blues" Patrick Wensink** — A hilarious double helix of country music and physics. **196 pages $11**

BB-125 **"Barbarian Beast Bitches of the Badlands" Carlton Mellick III** — Three prequels and sequels to *Warrior Wolf Women of the Wasteland*. **284 pages $13**

BB-126 **"The Traveling Dildo Salesman" Kevin L. Donihe** — A nightmare comedy about destiny, faith, and sex toys. Also featuring Donihe's most lurid and infamous short stories: *Milky Agitation, Two-Way Santa, The Helen Mower, Living Room Zombies,* and *Revenge of the Living Masturbation Rag.* **108 pages $8**

BB-127 **"Metamorphosis Blues" Bruce Taylor** — Enter a land of love beasts, intergalactic cowboys, and rock 'n roll. A land where Sears Catalogs are doorways to insanity and men keep mysterious black boxes. Welcome to the monstrous mind of Mr. Magic Realism. **136 pages $11**

BB-128 **"The Driver's Guide to Hitting Pedestrians" Andersen Prunty** — A pocket guide to the twenty-three most painful things in life, written by the most well-adjusted man in the universe. **108 pages $8**

BB-129 **"Island of the Super People" Kevin Shamel** — Four students and their anthropology professor journey to a remote island to study its indigenous population. But this is no ordinary native culture. They're super heroes and villains with flesh costumes and out-landish abilities like self-detonation, musical eyelashes, and microwave hands. **194 pages $11**

BB-130 **"Fantastic Orgy" Carlton Mellick III** — Shark Sex, mutant cats, and strange sexually transmitted diseases. Featuring the stories: *Candy-coated, Ear Cat, Fantastic Orgy, City Hobgoblins,* and *Porno in August.* **136 pages $9**

BB-131 **"Cripple Wolf" Jeff Burk** — Part man. Part wolf. 100% crippled. Also including *Punk Rock Nursing Home, Adrift with Space Badgers, Cook for Your Life, Just Another Day in the Park, Frosty and the Full Monty*, and *House of Cats.* **152 pages $10**

BB-132 **"I Knocked Up Satan's Daughter" Carlton Mellick III** — An adorable, violent, fantastical love story. A romantic comedy for the bizarro fiction reader. **152 pages $10**

BB-133 **"A Town Called Suckhole" David W. Barbee** — Far into the future, in the nuclear bowels of post-apocalyptic Dixie, there is a town. A town of derelict mobile homes, ancient junk, and mutant wildlife. A town of slack jawed rednecks who bask in the splendors of moonshine and mud boggin'. A town dedicated to the bloody and demented legacy of the Old South. A town called Suckhole. **144 pages $10**

BB-134 **"Cthulhu Comes to the Vampire Kingdom" Cameron Pierce** — What you'd get if H. P. Lovecraft wrote a Tim Burton animated film. **148 pages $11**

BB-135 **"I am Genghis Cum" Violet LeVoit** — From the savage Arctic tundra to post-partum mutations to your missing daughter's unmarked grave, join visionary madwoman Violet LeVoit in this non-stop eight-story onslaught of full-tilt Bizarro punk lit thrills. **124 pages $9**

BB-136 **"Haunt" Laura Lee Bahr** — A tripping-balls Los Angeles noir, where a mysterious dame drags you through a time-warping Bizarro hall of mirrors. **316 pages $13**

BB-137 **"Amazing Stories of the Flying Spaghetti Monster" edited by Cameron Pierce** — Like an all-spaghetti evening of Adult Swim, the Flying Spaghetti Monster will show you the many realms of His Noodly Appendage. Learn of those who worship him and the lives he touches in distant, mysterious ways. **228 pages $12**

BB-138 **"Wave of Mutilation" Douglas Lain** — A dream-pop exploration of modern architecture and the American identity, *Wave of Mutilation* is a Zen finger trap for the 21st century. **100 pages $8**

**BB-139 "Hooray for Death!" Mykle Hansen** — Famous Author Mykle Hansen draws unconventional humor from deaths tiny and large, and invites you to laugh while you can. **128 pages $10**

**BB-140 "Hypno-hog's Moonshine Monster Jamboree" Andrew Goldfarb** — Hicks, Hogs, Horror! Goldfarb is back with another strange illustrated tale of backwoods weirdness. **120 pages $9**

**BB-141 "Broken Piano For President" Patrick Wensink** — A comic masterpiece about the fast food industry, booze, and the necessity to choose happiness over work and security. **372 pages $15**

**BB-142 "Please Do Not Shoot Me in the Face" Bradley Sands** — A novel in three parts, *Please Do Not Shoot Me in the Face: A Novel*, is the story of one boy detective, the worst ninja in the world, and the great American fast food wars. It is a novel of loss, destruction, and--incredibly--genuine hope. **224 pages $12**

**BB-143 "Santa Steps Out" Robert Devereaux** — Sex, Death, and Santa Claus ... The ultimate erotic Christmas story is back. **294 pages $13**

**BB-144 "Santa Conquers the Homophobes" Robert Devereaux** — "I wish I could hope to ever attain one-thousandth the perversity of Robert Devereaux's toenail clippings." - Poppy Z. Brite **316 pages $13**

**BB-145 "We Live Inside You" Jeremy Robert Johnson** — "Jeremy Robert Johnson is dancing to a way different drummer. He loves language, he loves the edge, and he loves us people. These stories have range and style and wit. This is entertainment... and literature."- Jack Ketchum **188 pages $11**

**BB-146 "Clockwork Girl" Athena Villaverde** — Urban fairy tales for the weird girl in all of us. Like a combination of Francesca Lia Block, Charles de Lint, Kathe Koja, Tim Burton, and Hayao Miyazaki, her stories are cute, kinky, edgy, magical, provocative, and strange, full of poetic imagery and vicious sexuality. **160 pages $10**

BB-147 **"Armadillo Fists" Carlton Mellick III** — A weird-as-hell gangster story set in a world where people drive giant mechanical dinosaurs instead of cars. **168 pages $11**

BB-148 **"Gargoyle Girls of Spider Island" Cameron Pierce** — Four college seniors venture out into open waters for the tropical party weekend of a lifetime. Instead of a teenage sex fantasy, they find themselves in a nightmare of pirates, sharks, and sex-crazed monsters. **100 pages $8**

BB-149 **"The Handsome Squirm" by Carlton Mellick III** — Like Franz Kafka's *The Trial* meets an erotic body horror version of *The Blob*. **158 pages $11**

BB-150 **"Tentacle Death Trip" Jordan Krall** — It's *Death Race 2000* meets H. P. Lovecraft in bizarro author Jordan Krall's best and most suspenseful work to date. **224 pages $12**

BB-151 **"The Obese" Nick Antosca** — Like Alfred Hitchcock's *The Birds*... but with obese people. **108 pages $10**

BB-152 **"All-Monster Action!" Cody Goodfellow** — The world gave him a blank check and a demand: Create giant monsters to fight our wars. But Dr. Otaku was not satisfied with mere chaos and mass destruction.... **216 pages $12**

BB-153 **"Ugly Heaven" Carlton Mellick III** — Heaven is no longer a paradise. It was once a blissful utopia full of wonders far beyond human comprehension. But the afterlife is now in ruins. It has become an ugly, lonely wasteland populated by strange monstrous beasts, masturbating angels, and sad man-like beings wallowing in the remains of the once-great Kingdom of God. **106 pages $8**

BB-154 **"Space Walrus" Kevin L. Donihe** — Walter is supposed to go where no walrus has ever gone before, but all this astronaut walrus really wants is to take it easy on the intense training, escape the chimpanzee bullies, and win the love of his human trainer Dr. Stephanie. **160 pages $11**

Lightning Source UK Ltd.
Milton Keynes UK
UKHW011916210223
417406UK00001B/139